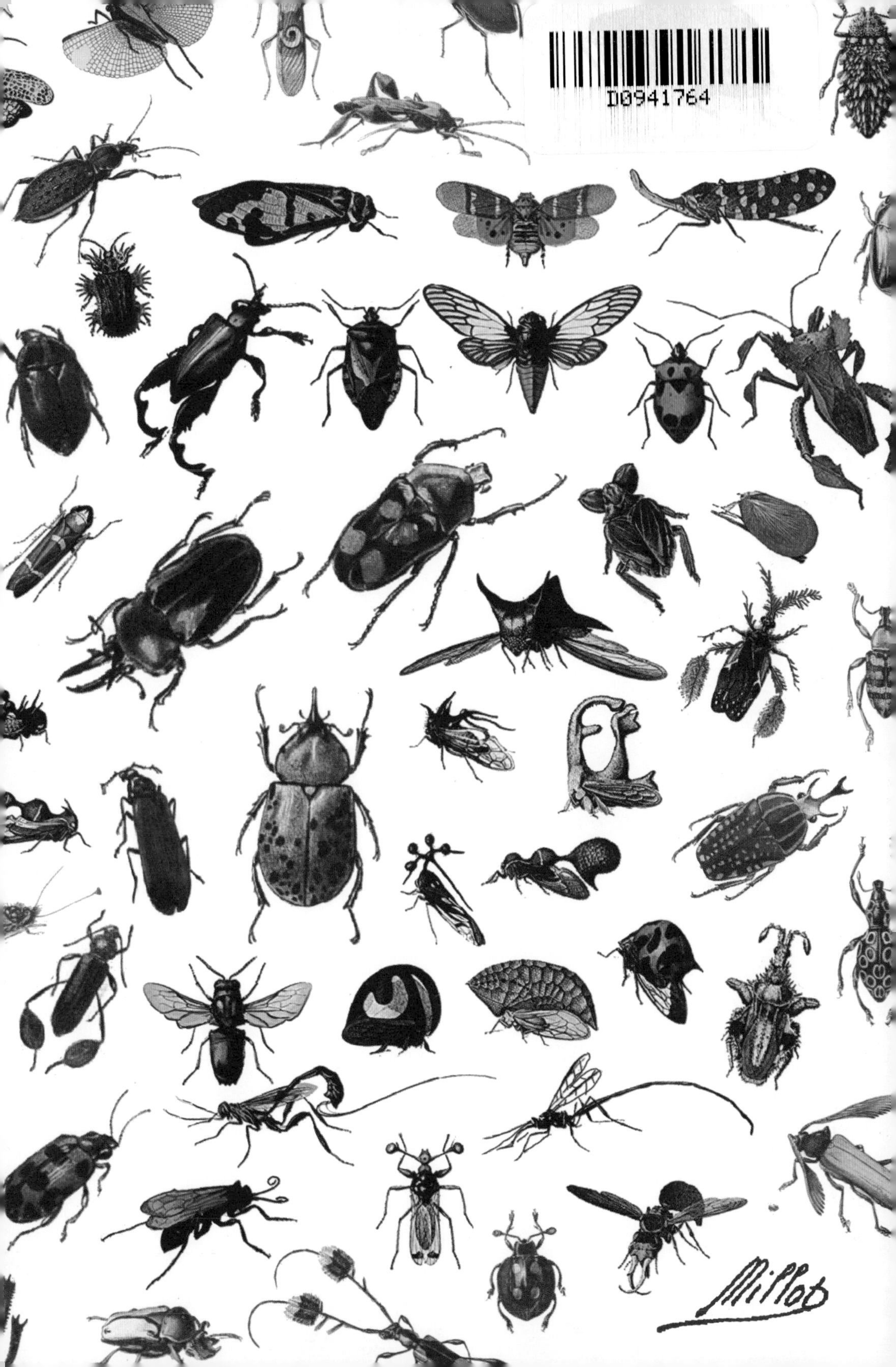
Millot

drawnandquarterly.com | elisegravel.com

ISBN 978-1-77046-415-5
First edition: August 2021
Printed in China | 10 9 8 7 6 5 4 3 2 1

Cataloguing data available from Library and Archives Canada.

Published in the USA by Drawn & Quarterly, a client publisher of Farrar, Straus and Giroux.
Published in Canada by Drawn & Quarterly, a client publisher of Raincoast Books.
Published in the United Kingdom by Drawn & Quarterly, a client publisher of Publishers Group UK.

Canada ▮◆▮ Drawn & Quarterly acknowledges the support of the Government of Canada and the Canada Council for the Arts for our publishing program.

Drawn & Quarterly reconnaît l'aide financière du gouvernement du Québec par l'entremise de la Société de développement des entreprises culturelles (SODEC) pour nos activités d'édition. Gouvernement du Québec—Programme de crédit d'impôt pour l'édition de livres—Gestion SODEC.

ELISE GRAVEL

DRAWN & QUARTERLY

I have

ALWAYS

been fascinated by bugs.

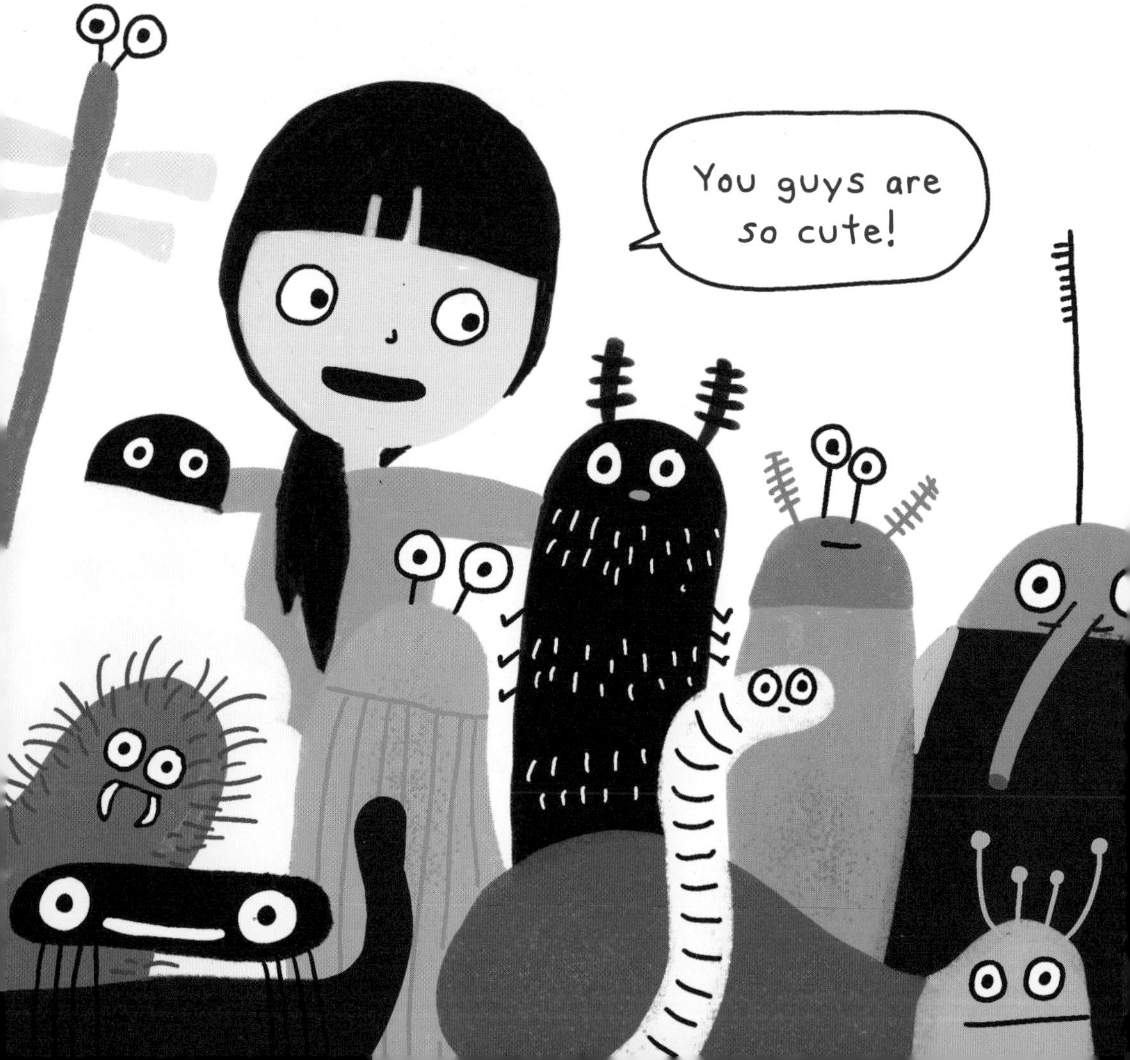
You guys are so cute!

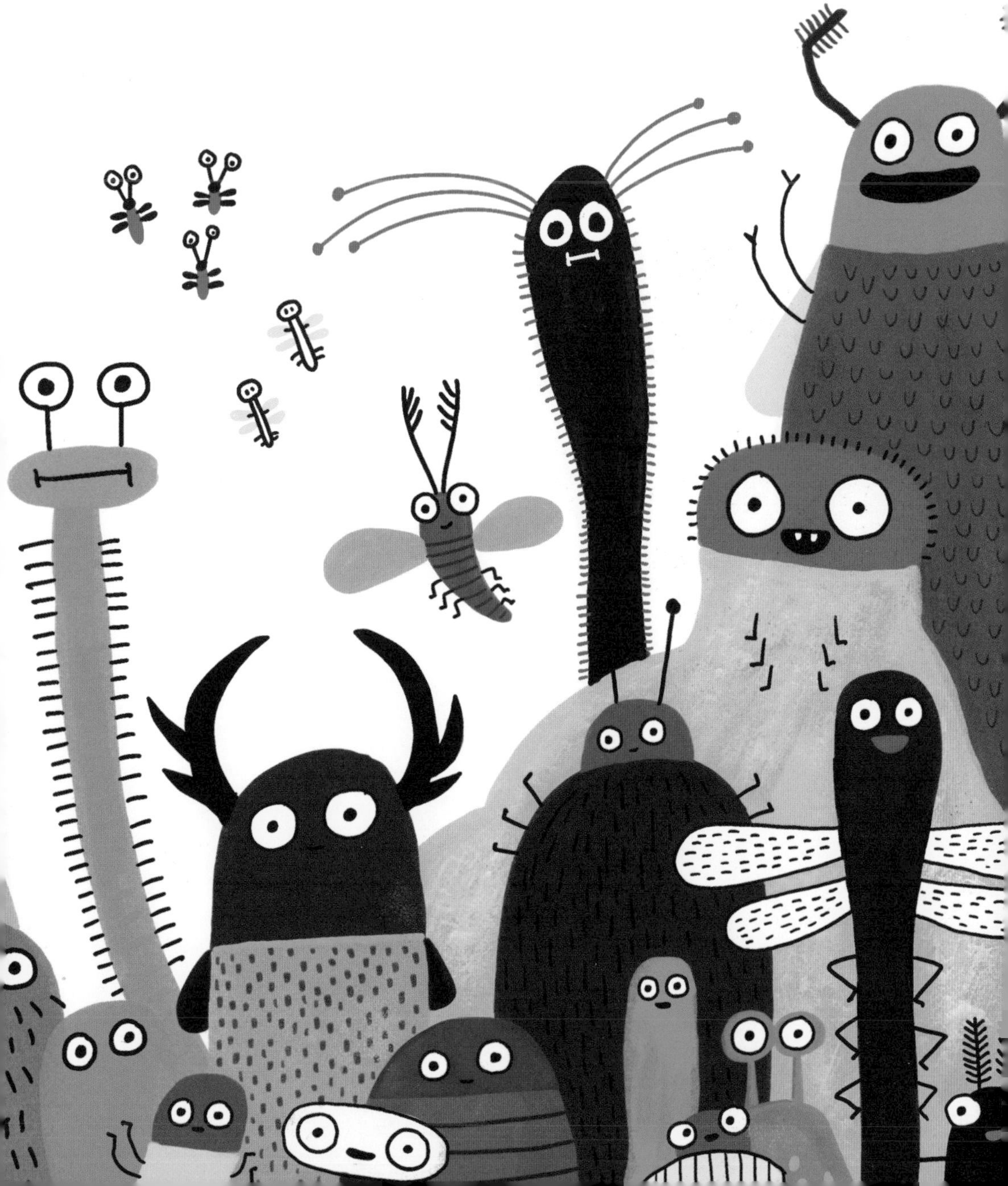

As a kid, observing them was one of my favourite activities. I looked for them everywhere. It was probably pretty annoying for them. Sorry, bugs.

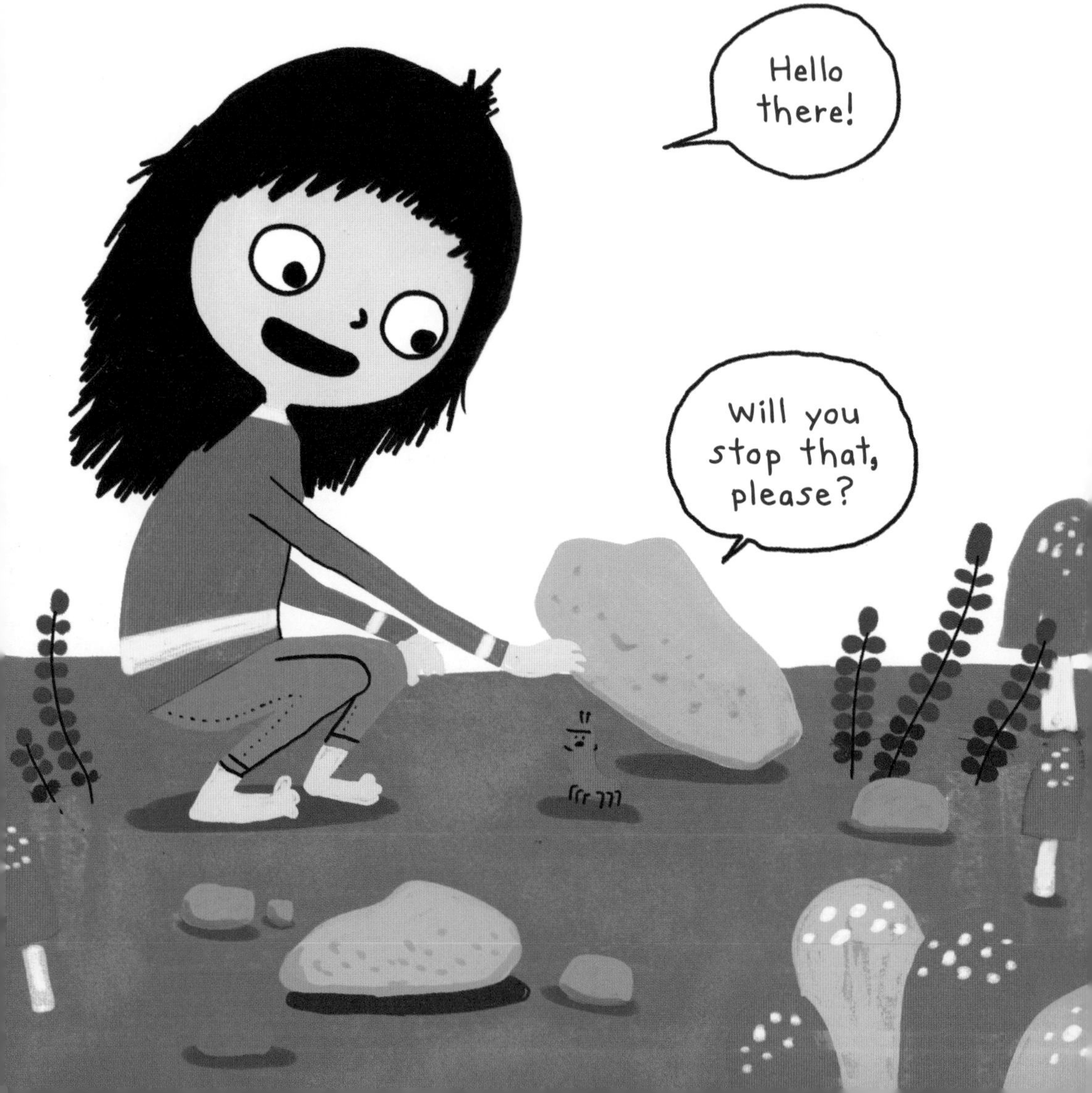
Hello there!
Will you stop that, please?

On top of being cute and fascinating, bugs are extremely

IMPORTANT

for the health of our planet.

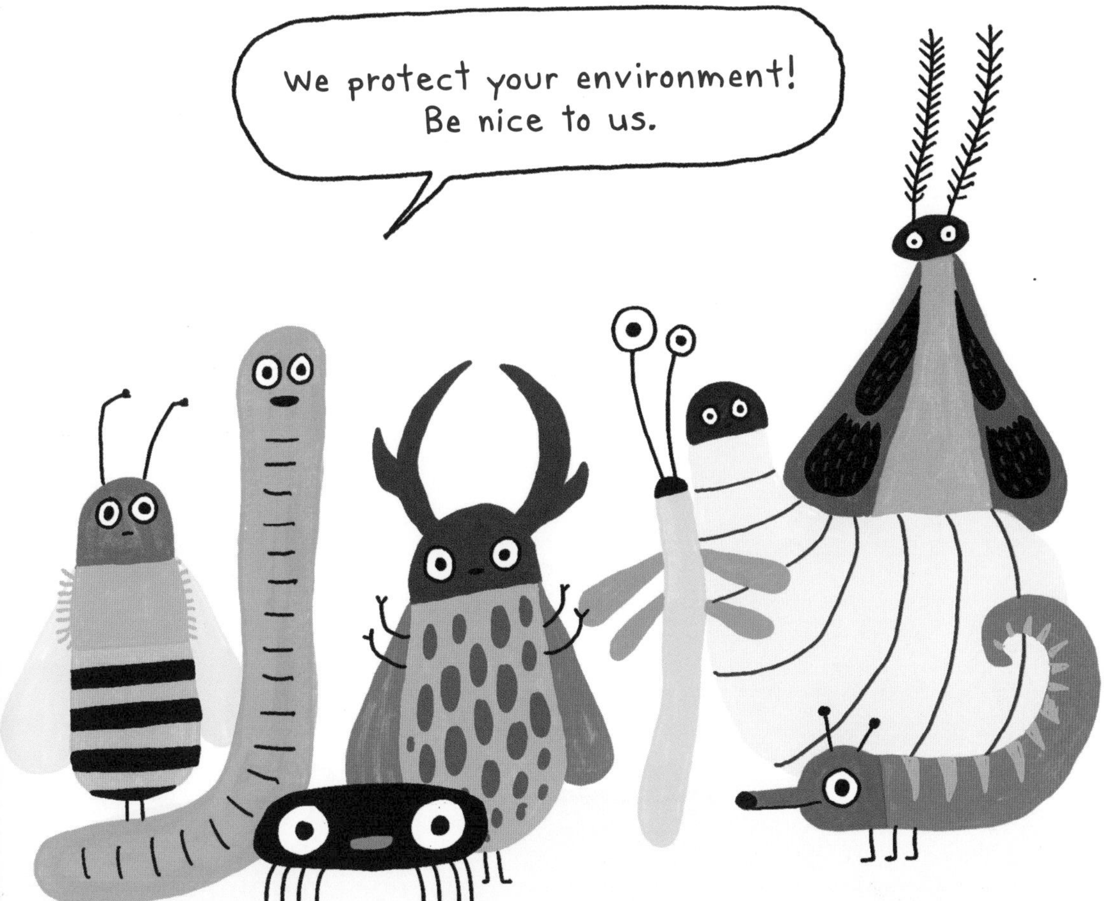
We protect your environment!
Be nice to us.

The creatures we call bugs are part of a big group of animals called

INVERTEBRATES.

Here are some animals from that group.

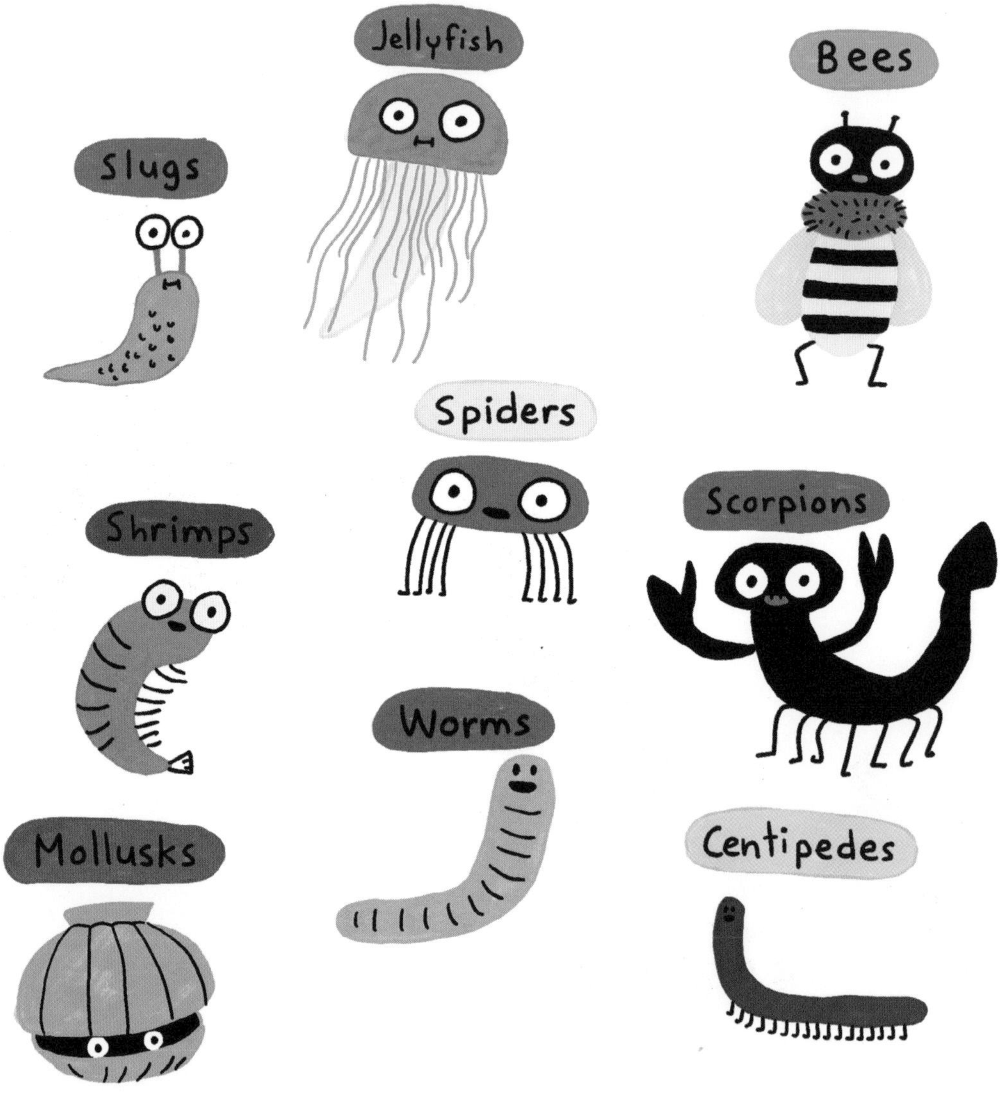
Jellyfish
Bees
Slugs
Spiders
Shrimps
Scorpions
Worms
Mollusks
Centipedes

When we use the word **INSECT**

we're talking about invertebrates who are roughly shaped like this guy:

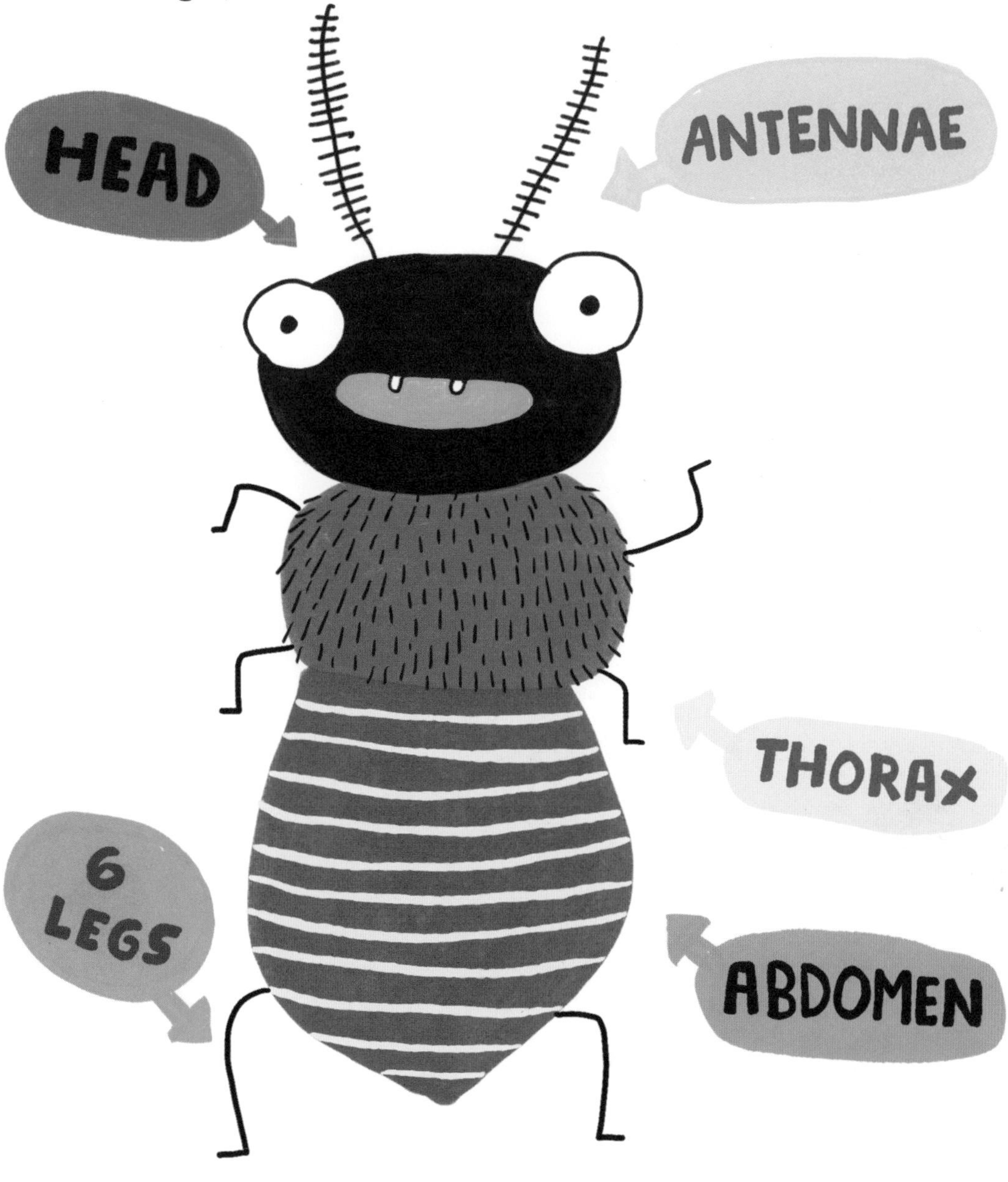
HEAD
ANTENNAE
THORAX
6 LEGS
ABDOMEN

(Disclaimer: I don't draw very realistic insects)

The scientists who study insects are called

ENTOMOLOGISTS.

When I was a kid, I thought I would become one.
I became an artist instead, but I still think I'd
love being an entomologist.

Will you sit still and
let me study you?

Unlike many grownups, I

LOVE BUGS!

Let me tell you a bit about why I
find them so interesting.

BUGS ARE WEIRD.

First of all, I like most weird creatures, and bugs are among the weirdest creatures on our planet. Look at the fly head I drew on the next page. Now just imagine meeting one of these, but human-sized. Wouldn't you totally think you've just met an alien?

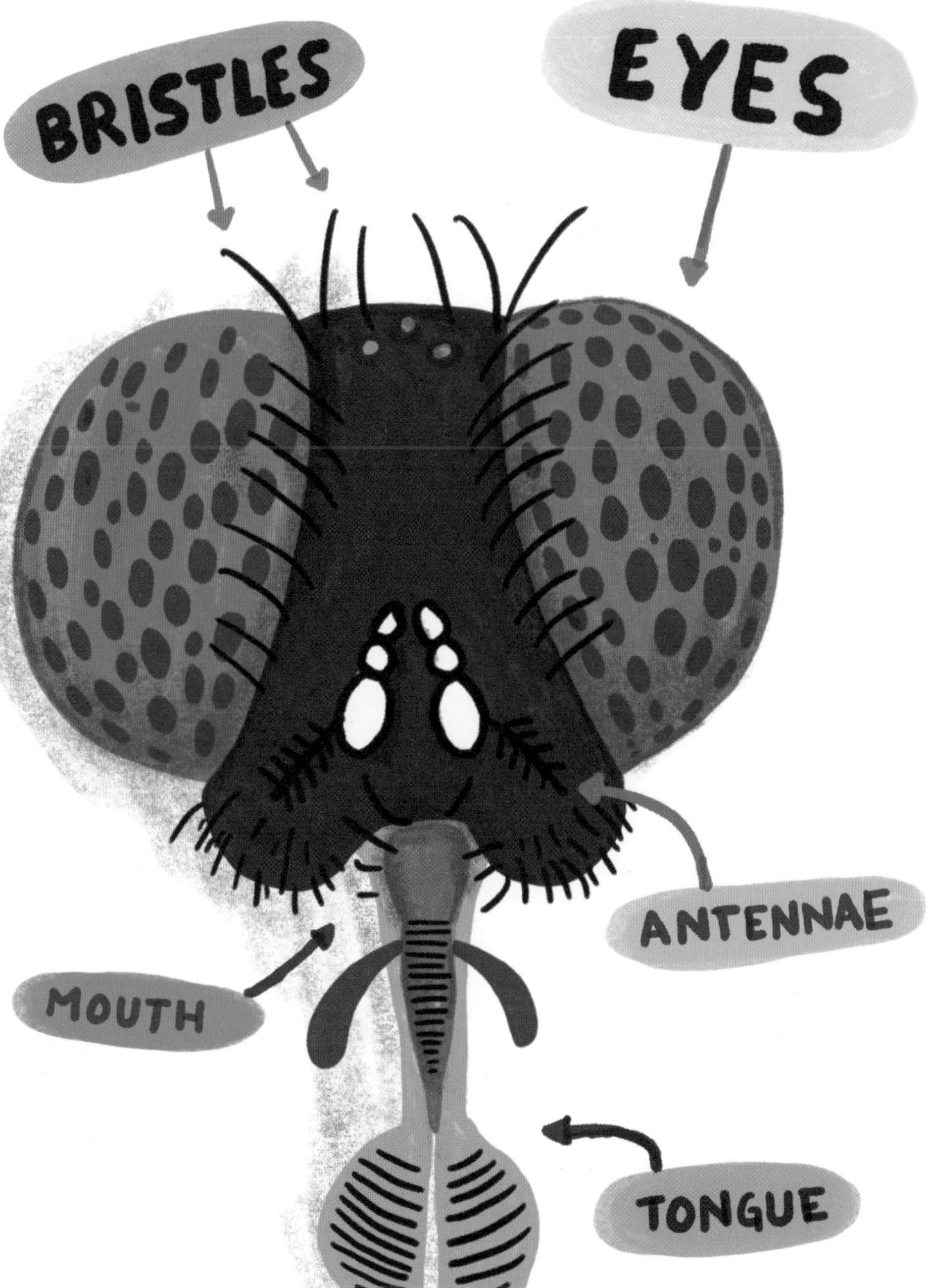
BRISTLES
EYES
ANTENNAE
MOUTH
TONGUE

Antenna Shapes

Here, I've drawn a bunch of different antennae and insect wings, just for fun. Aren't they pretty?

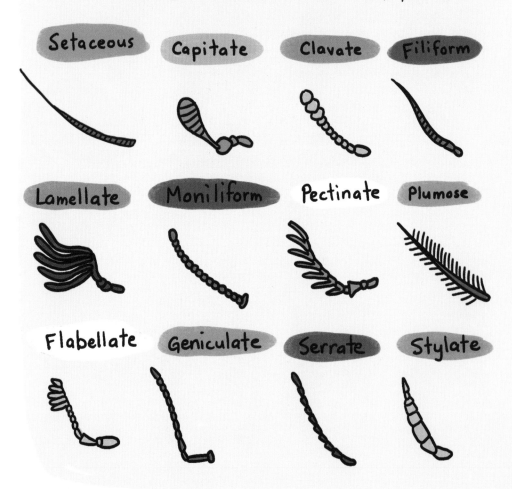

Setaceous
Capitate
Clavate
Filiform
Lamellate
Moniliform
Pectinate
Plumose
Flabellate
Geniculate
Serrate
Stylate

Wing Shapes

THE LIFE OF AN INSECT

Most bugs hatch from eggs. They then become larvae (which are like babies), then pupae (or cocoons, these are like teenagers), and finally, adult bugs. Here's a drawing of a butterfly's life cycle.

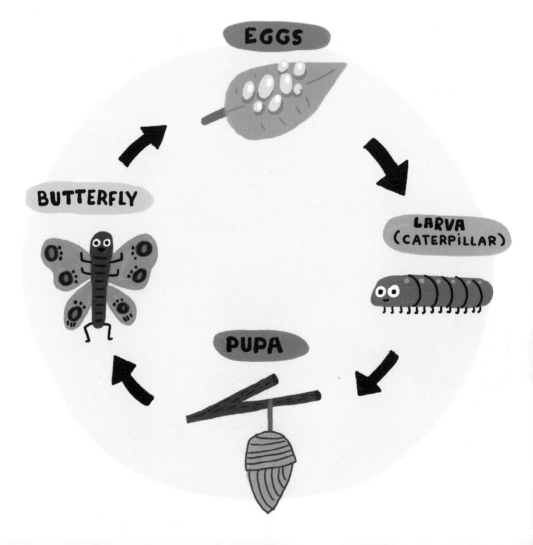

EGGS

LARVA
(CATERPILLAR)

PUPA

BUTTERFLY

Most baby bugs don't look at all like their mamas.

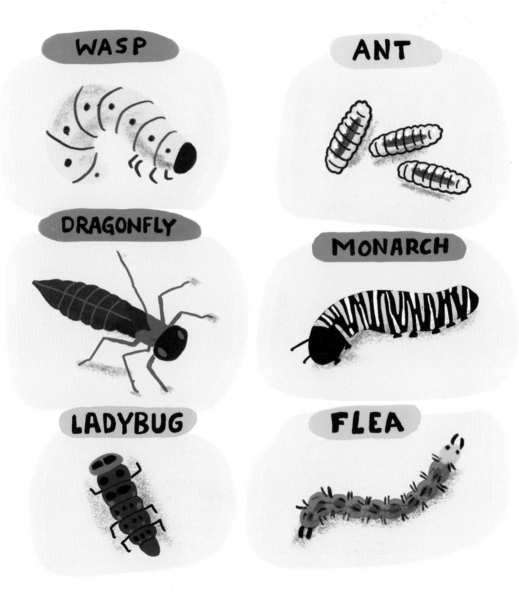

WASP

ANT

DRAGONFLY

MONARCH

LADYBUG

FLEA

There are millions of bug species, and scientists think that there are around

10 QUINTILLION

total bugs on Earth.

That's 1, 000, 000, 000, 000, 000, 000 bugs.

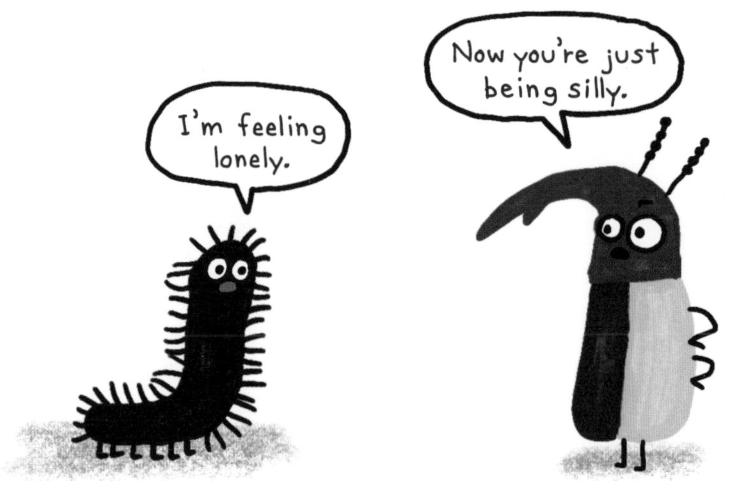

I'm feeling lonely.
Now you're just being silly.

If we weighed all the humans and bugs on the planet, the weight of the bugs would be seventy times greater than the weight of humans.

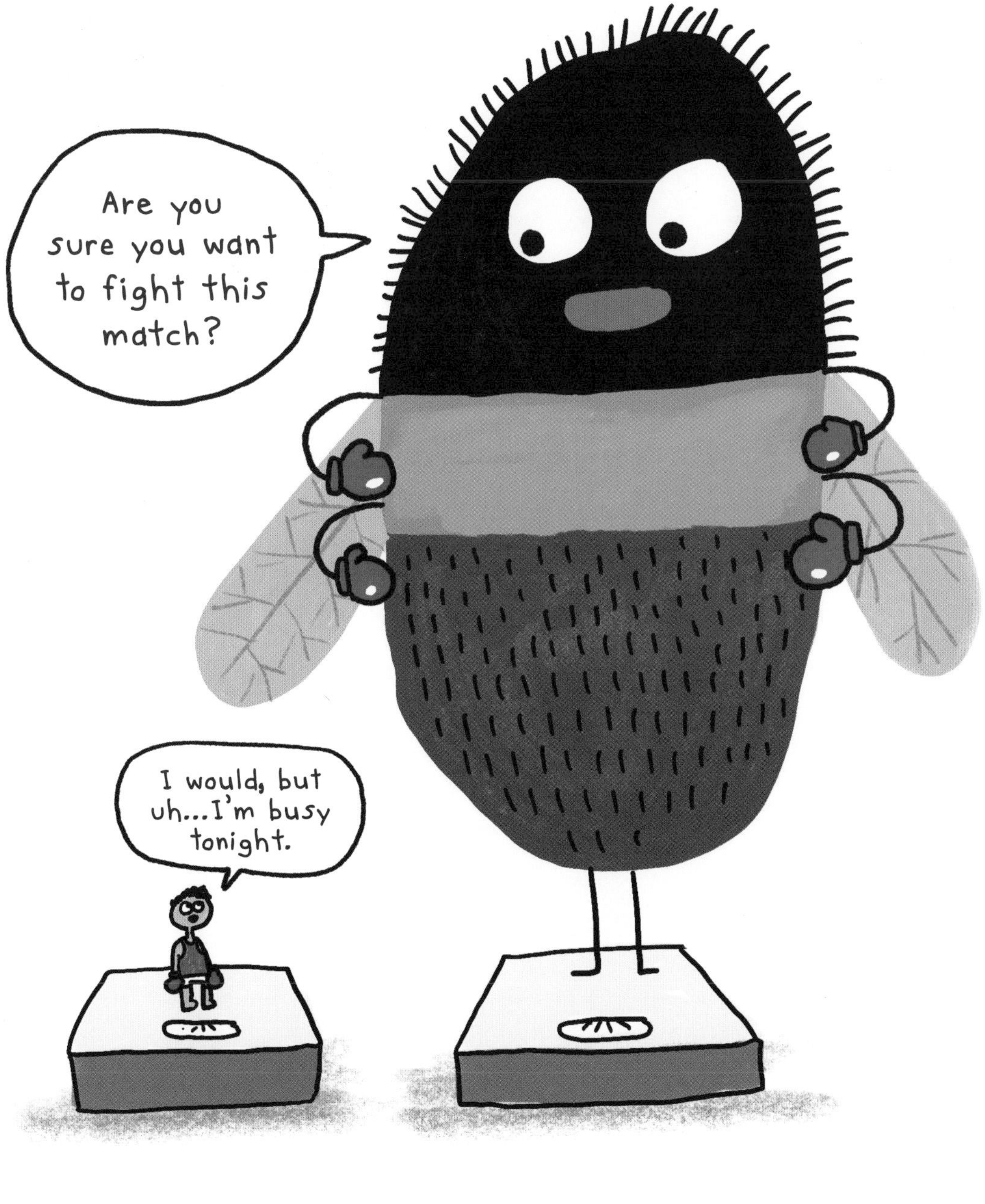
Are you sure you want to fight this match?
I would, but uh...I'm busy tonight.

THE STICK INSECT

Here's one of my favourite bugs. They are also called the WALKING STICK. They look almost exactly like a twig, which is excellent camouflage from animals who would like to eat them.

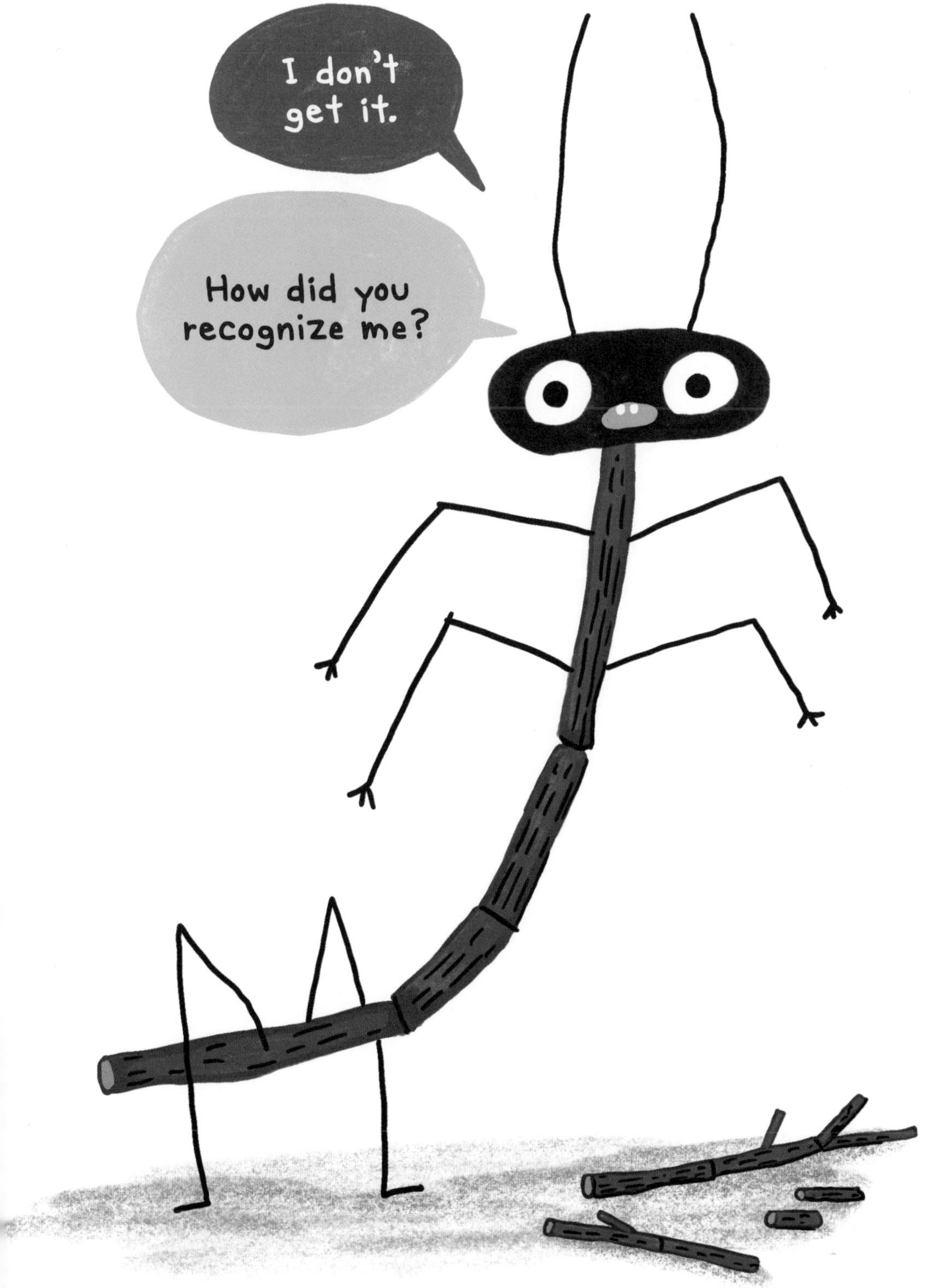
I don't get it.
How did you recognize me?

THE PILL BUG

This little guy *is* amazing. We call them bugs, but in fact, they are a lot more similar to shrimp than insects. They are a crustacean.

If you see one, touch them very gently and they'll transform into a marble before your eyes! That's what they do to protect themself when they feel threatened.

Other fun facts about pill bugs: they don't need to pee, they often eat their own poop, and they can eat metal.

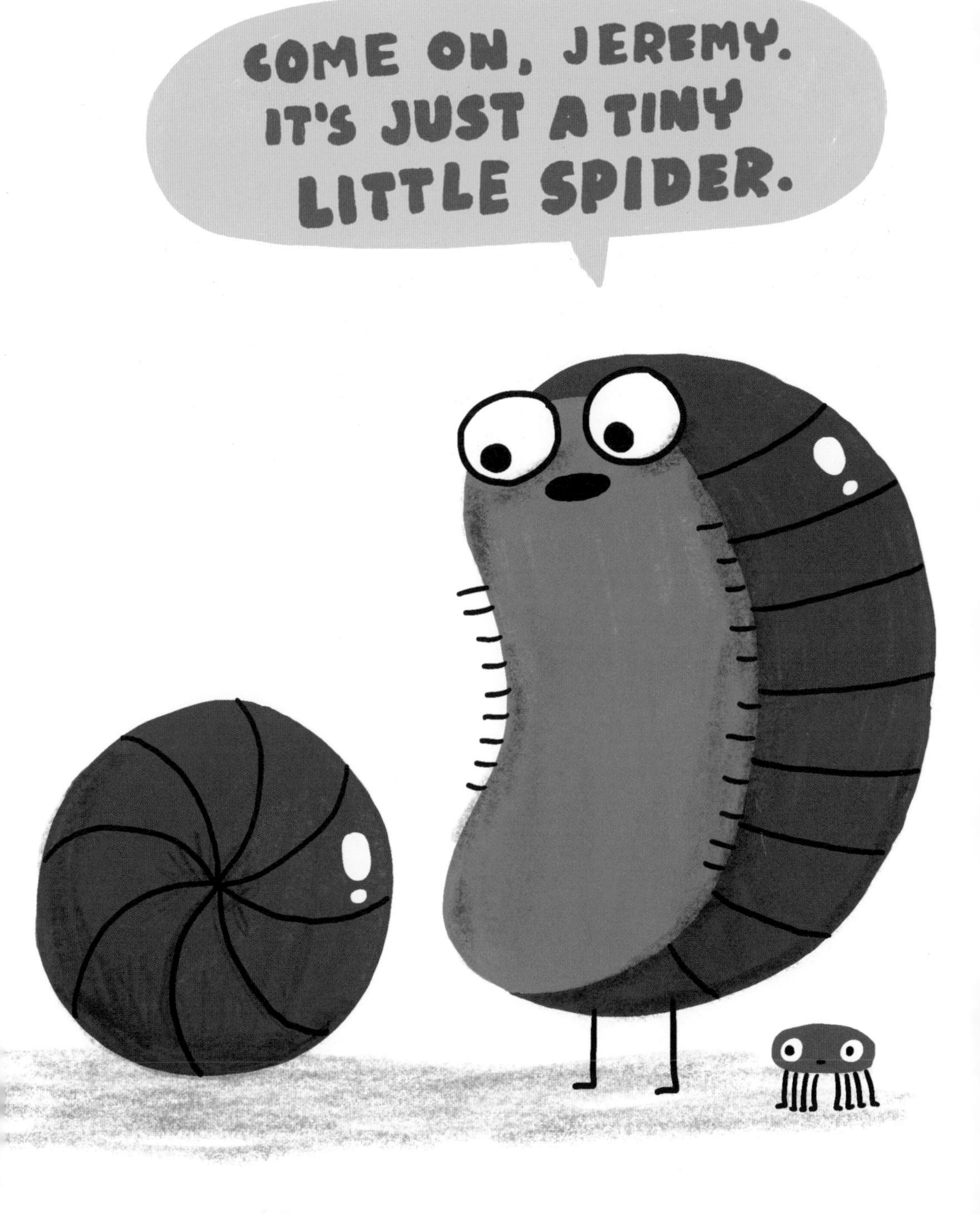
COME ON, JEREMY. IT'S JUST A TINY LITTLE SPIDER.

THE SCORPION FLY

I wanted to draw this creature because
they're pretty scary! Their scorpion-like tail
looks dangerous, but really it's harmless:
the scorpion fly doesn't sting.

Fun fact: when a male scorpion fly wants to
impress a female scorpion fly, he presents her
with a dead insect or with a drop of spit.
How thoughtful of him.

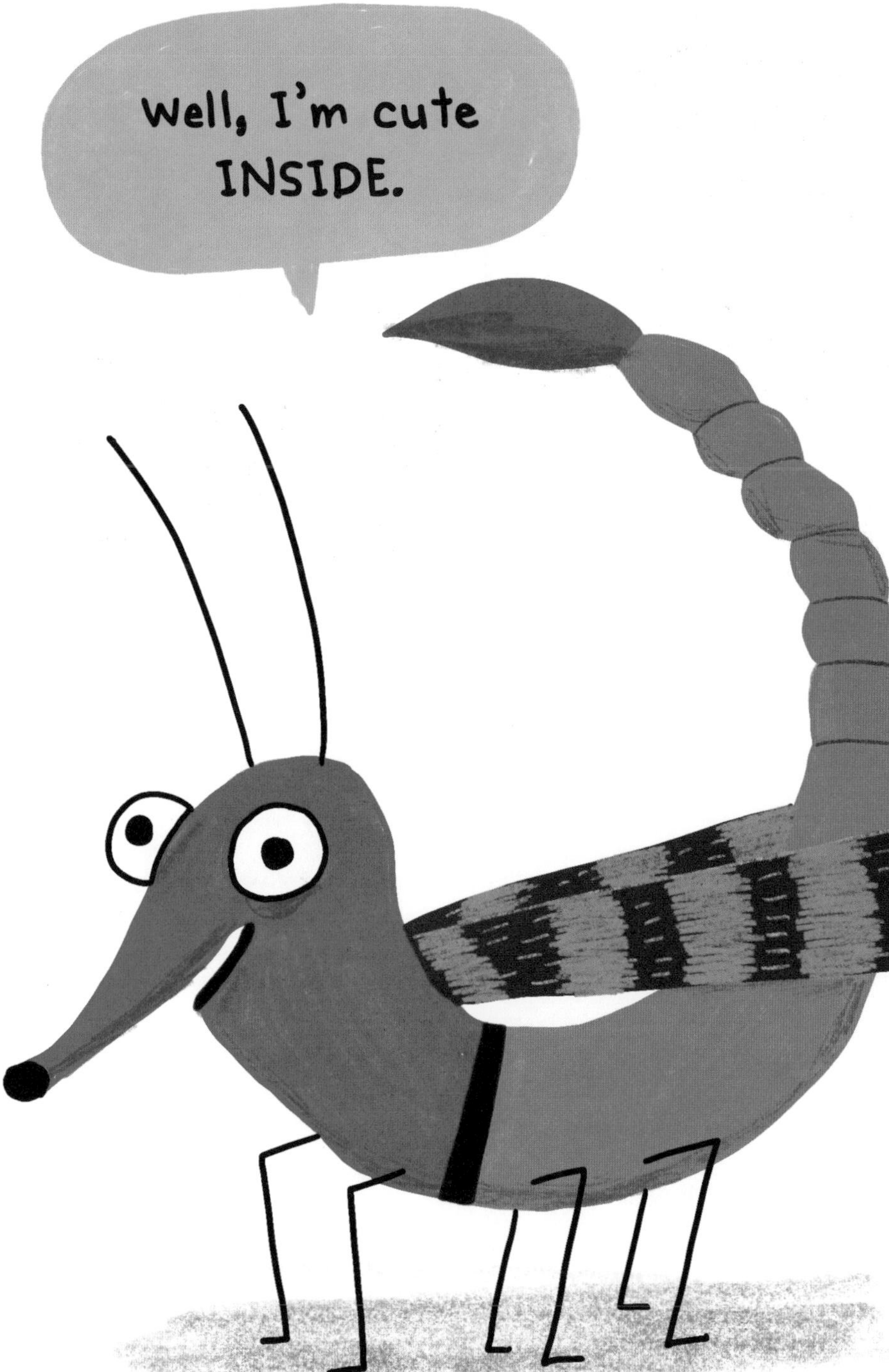
Well, I'm cute INSIDE.

THE STINK BUG

Stink bugs are shaped like shields.
And can you guess where their name
comes from? You're right: they stink!

When they are afraid, they release a
disgusting odour to repel their enemy.
Some people say that stink bugs smell
like sweaty feet and cilantro.
    Yummy!

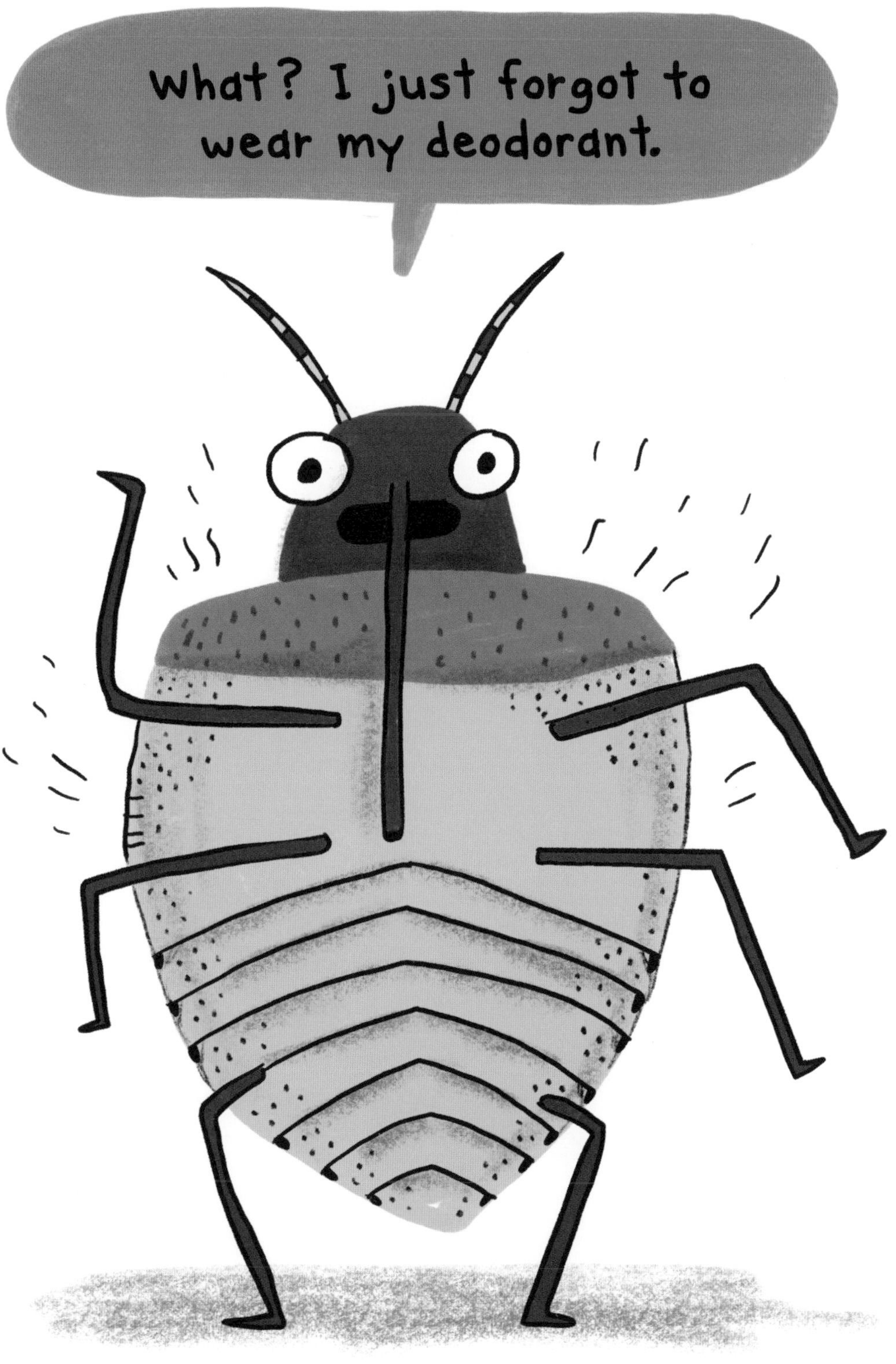
What? I just forgot to wear my deodorant.

THE PRAYING MANTIS

This strange insect is a master of disguise: they're very hard to spot when they're hiding among plants. They're terrifying hunters, and will only eat <u>live</u> insects and even small birds.

The praying mantis is the only insect that can turn its head. I saw one once. It turned to look at me. I have to admit that I screamed and ran away. We are lucky praying mantises are not human-sized.

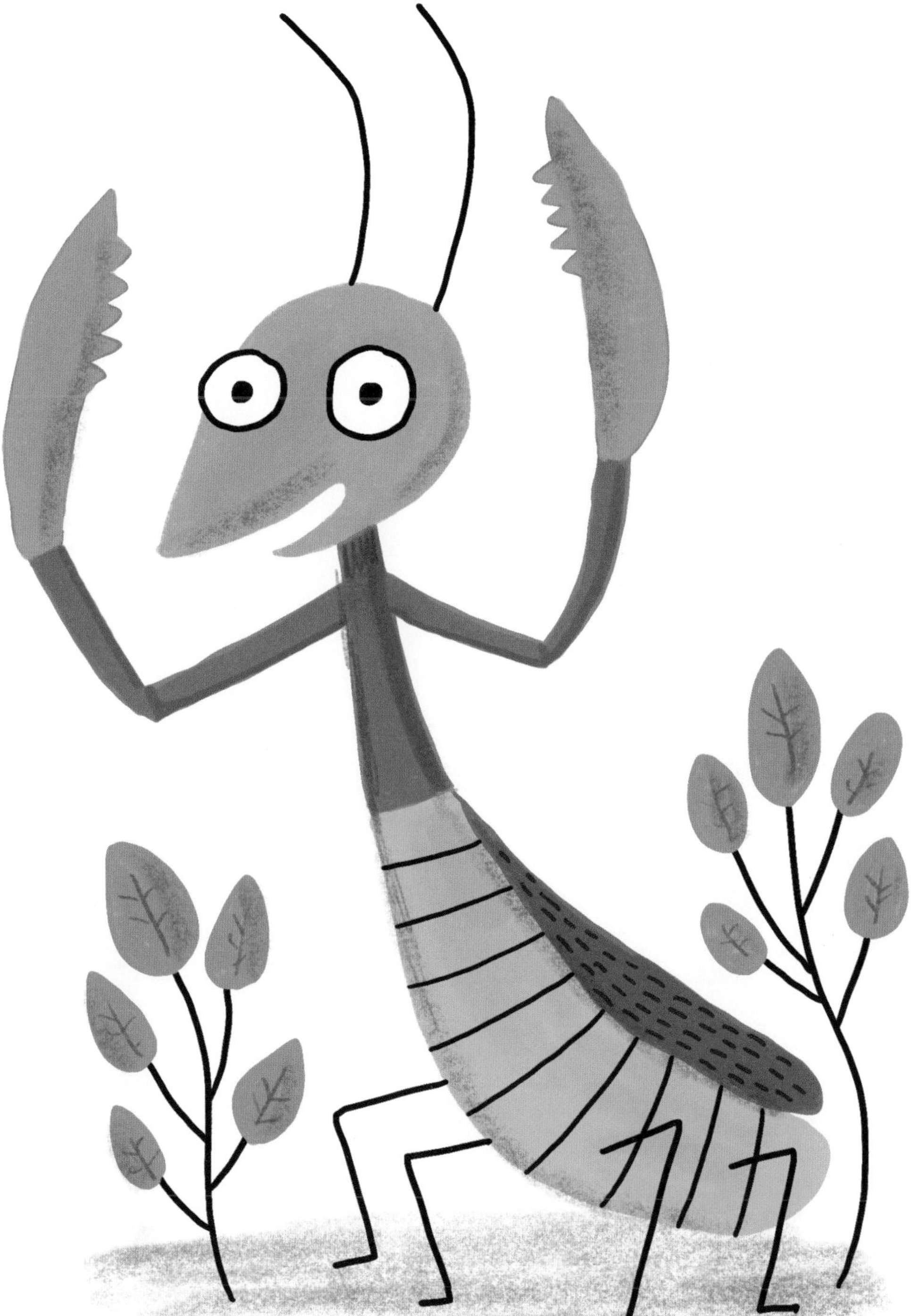

I love to draw underground scenes, so here are a bunch of bugs that live in soil and under rocks. Don't they look cozy down there?

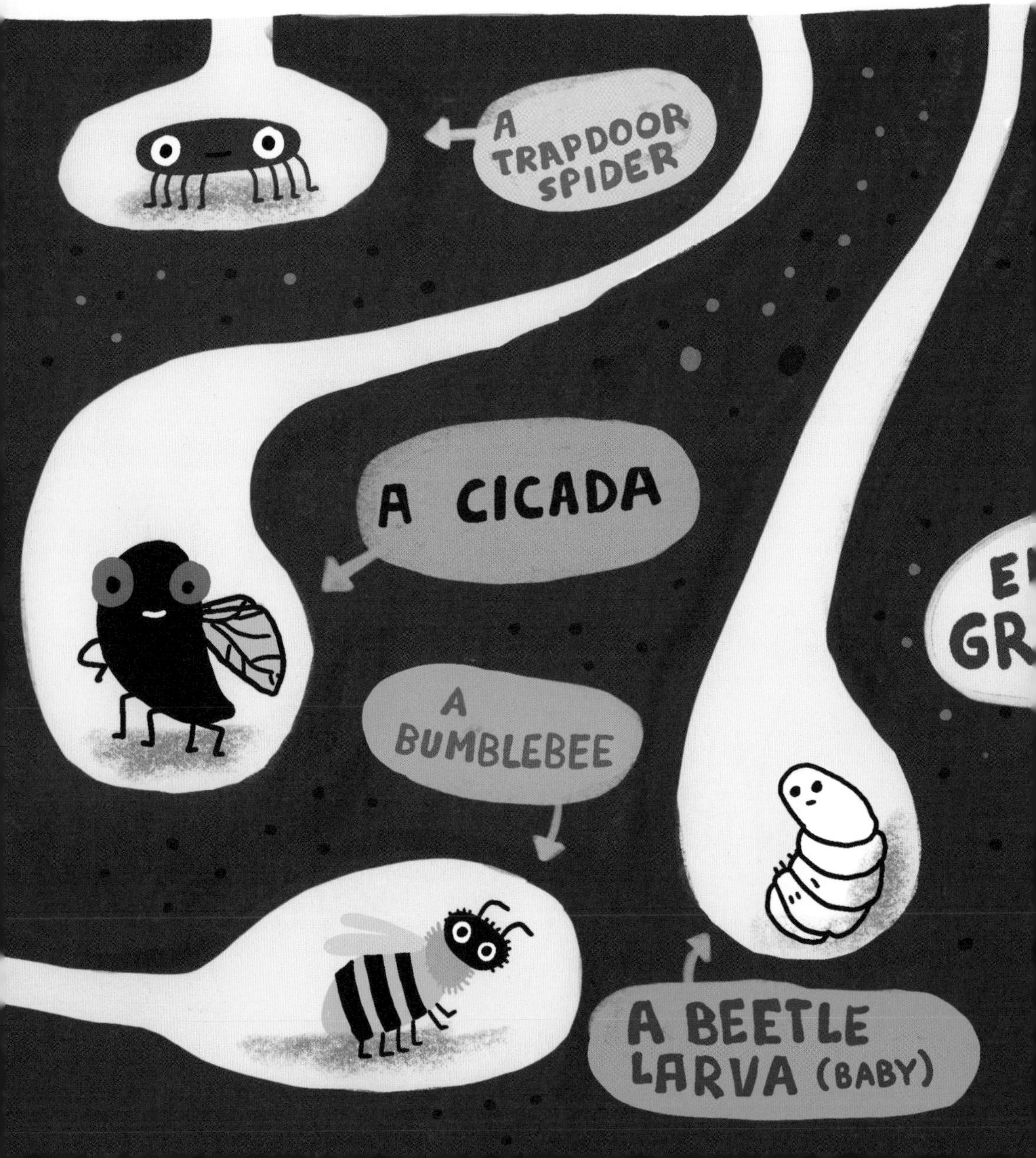
A TRAPDOOR SPIDER
A CICADA
A BUMBLEBEE
A BEETLE LARVA (BABY)

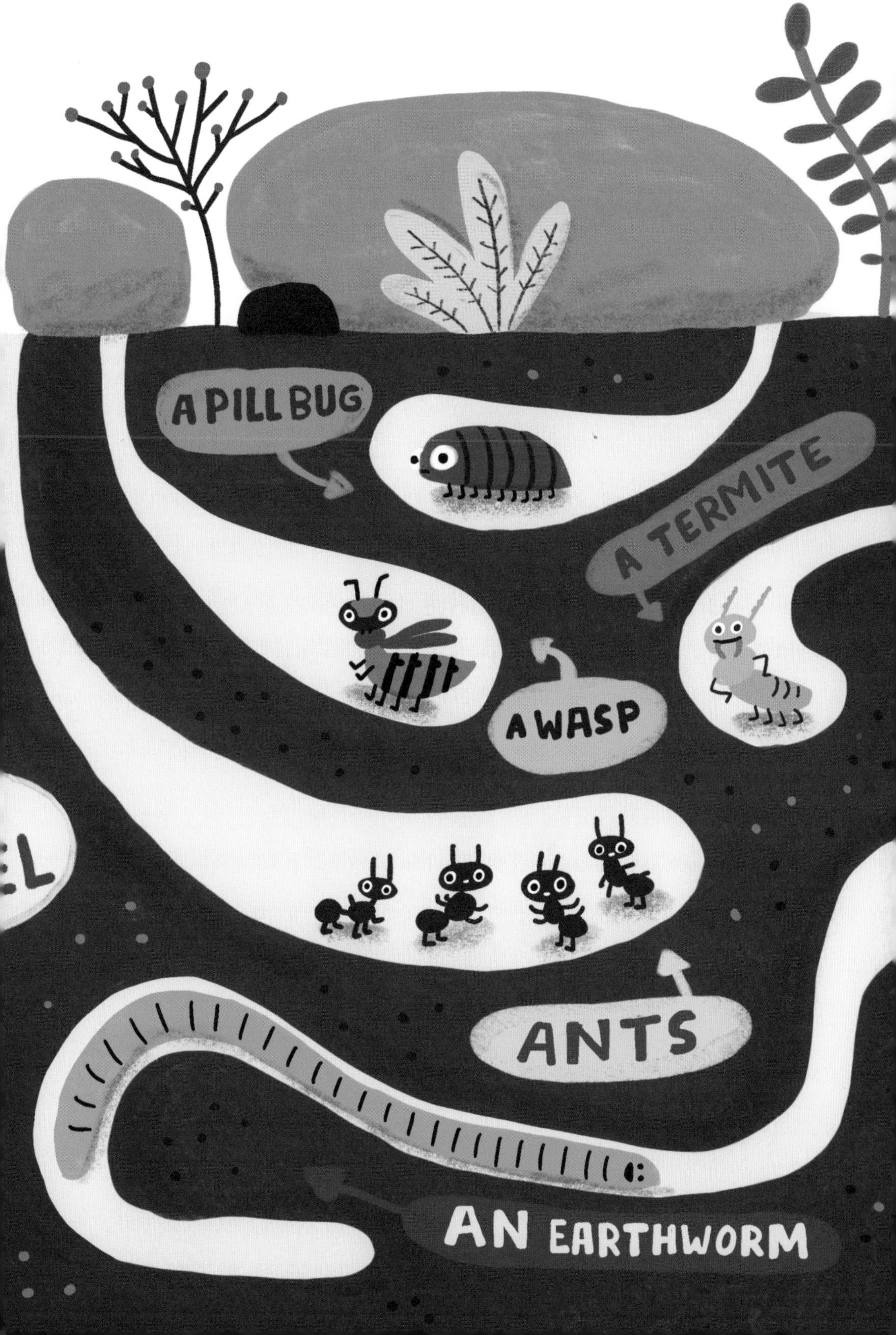

A PILL BUG
A TERMITE
A WASP
ANTS
AN EARTHWORM

THE TARDIGRADE

Here's one of my favourite tiny animals ever, although I've never seen one with my own eyes. You probably won't either. That's because the tardigrade, also called the waterbear, is microscopic.

I love tardigrades because they're tough as nails: they can survive in environments that would certainly kill us! Scientists discovered that they can stay alive in extremely cold and hot temperatures, and also in outer space. They can also survive ten years without water and thirty years frozen!

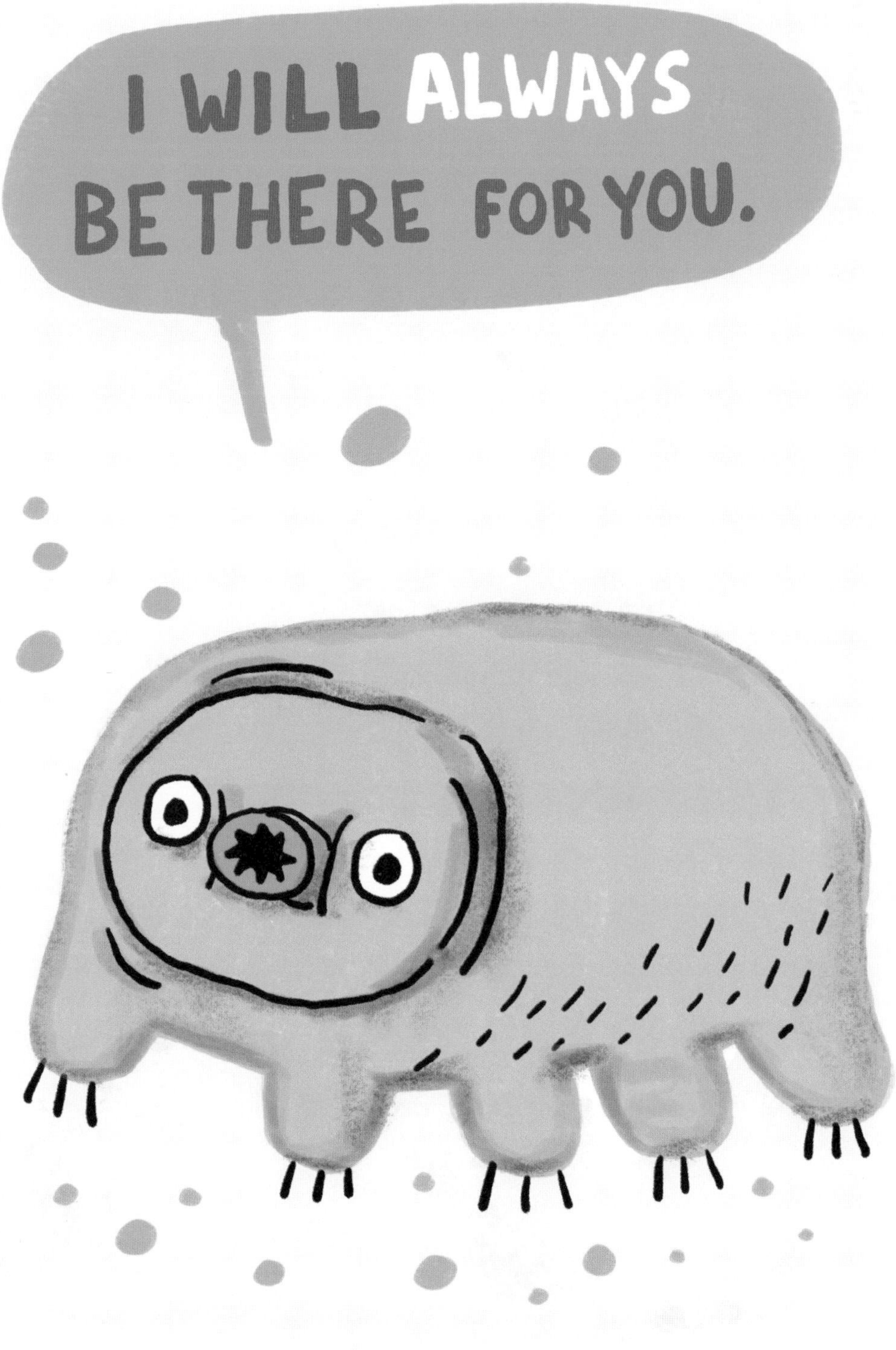
I WILL ALWAYS BE THERE FOR YOU.

THE LESSERBLACK TARANTULA

This tarantula looks like other tarantulas: it's a big, hairy spider, and most people don't want to find it crawling in their bed at night.

The reason why I love this one? They keep PETS! Well, one pet: a tiny little frog. The lesserblack tarantula protects the frog because the frog eats all the little bugs that might destroy the tarantula's eggs. They help each other.

I find this pair adorable, don't you?

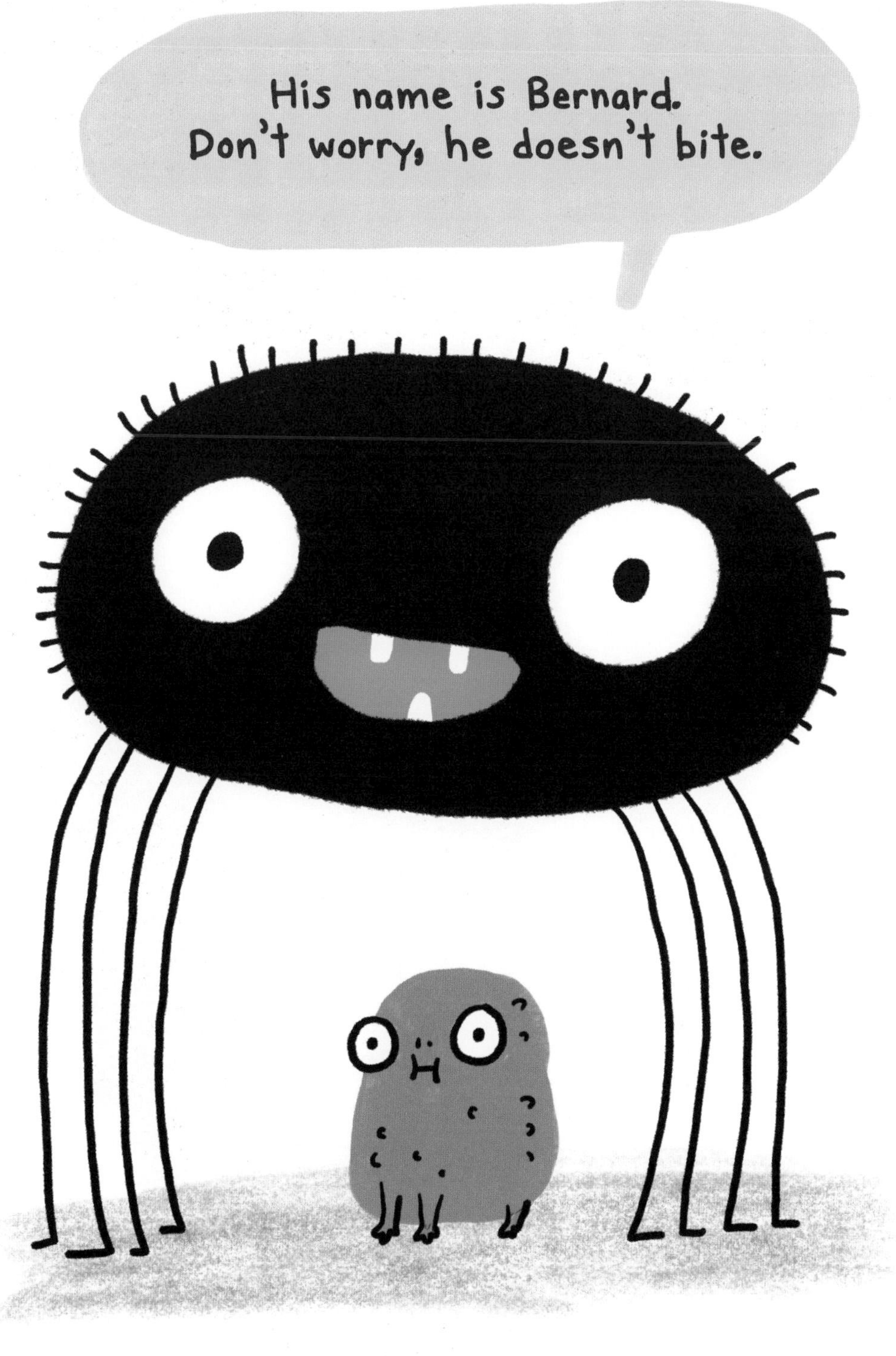
His name is Bernard.
Don't worry, he doesn't bite.

THE GIRAFFE WEEVIL

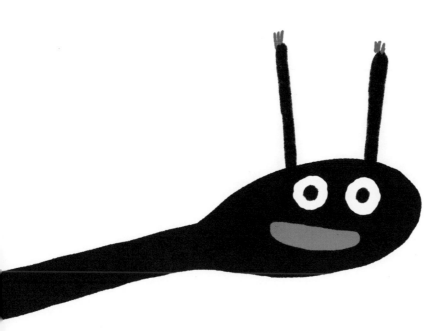

I had to draw this little insect because,
seriously, have you ever seen a cuter critter?
They're called the giraffe weevil because of—
you guessed it—their long neck.

The males have the longest necks, which
they use to fight each other: they try to
push each other off branches.

The female lays her egg on a leaf, which she
then carefully folds into a little pouch so
the larva can be all safe and cozy.

THE BEETLES

I'm in love with beetles. They are the prettiest insects of all;
I'd even say they are prettier than butterflies. But that's
just my personal taste, and I sometimes have weird tastes.
There are many, many kinds of beetles. Some of them look
like jewellery. They can be colourful, shiny, and bright.
Which one is your favourite?

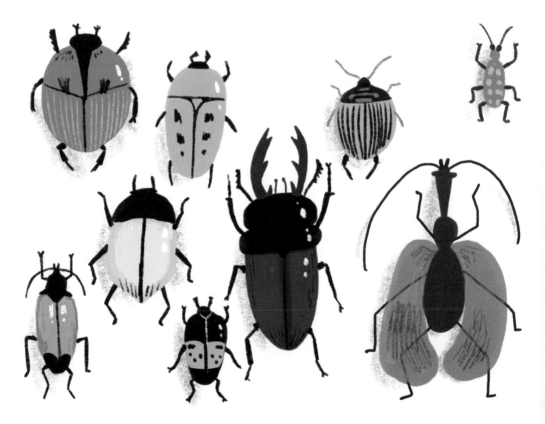

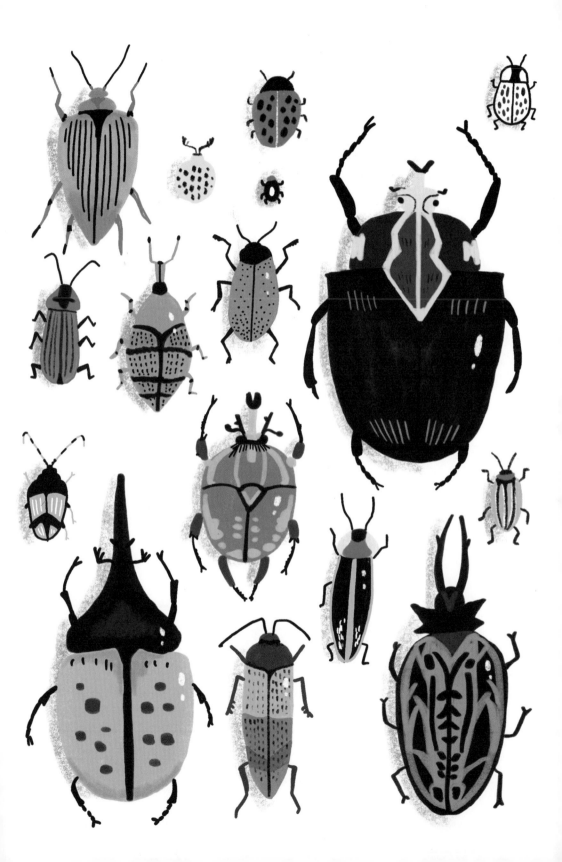

THE DUNG BEETLE

This one is a pretty fun beetle. They eat poop. The one I drew here is a roller dung beetle, which means they roll their provision of poop in a big ball that they can push around. They will bury it somewhere to eat as a snack later, or for the female to lay her eggs in.

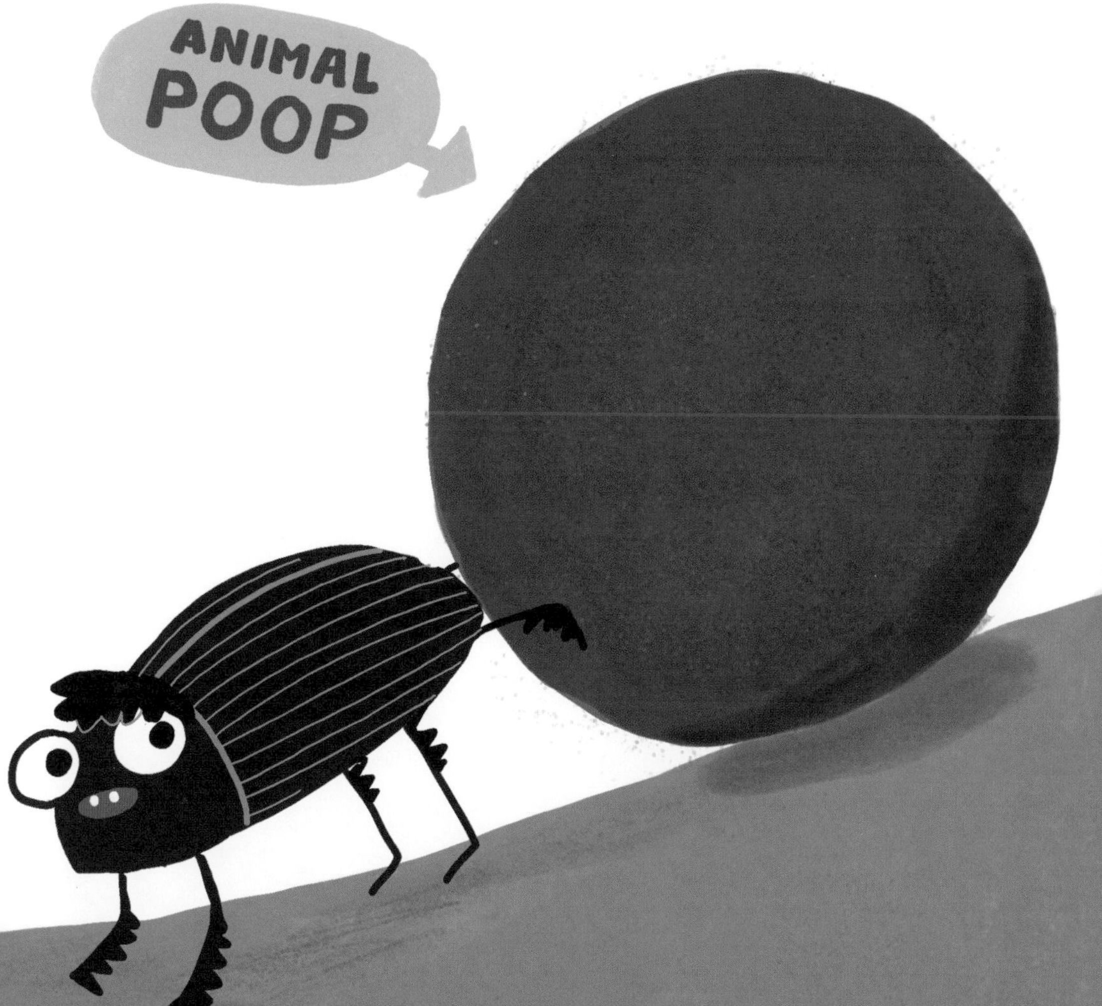
ANIMAL POOP

The dung beetle might be tiny, but in relation to their size, they're the strongest insect on Earth! They can push around a ball that's 1,000 times their own weight.

If you were as strong as a dung beetle, you would be able to drag six double-decker buses along the road.

THE HERCULES BEETLE

This beauty is one of the largest beetles; they can be as long as 6.7 inches! They live in tropical forests and hide in rotting tree trunks. They eat dead plants, leaves, and fruit. They use their huge horns in fights with other male beetles.

The Hercules beetle was once thought to be the strongest insect on the planet, but I guess you know who holds the record now, right?

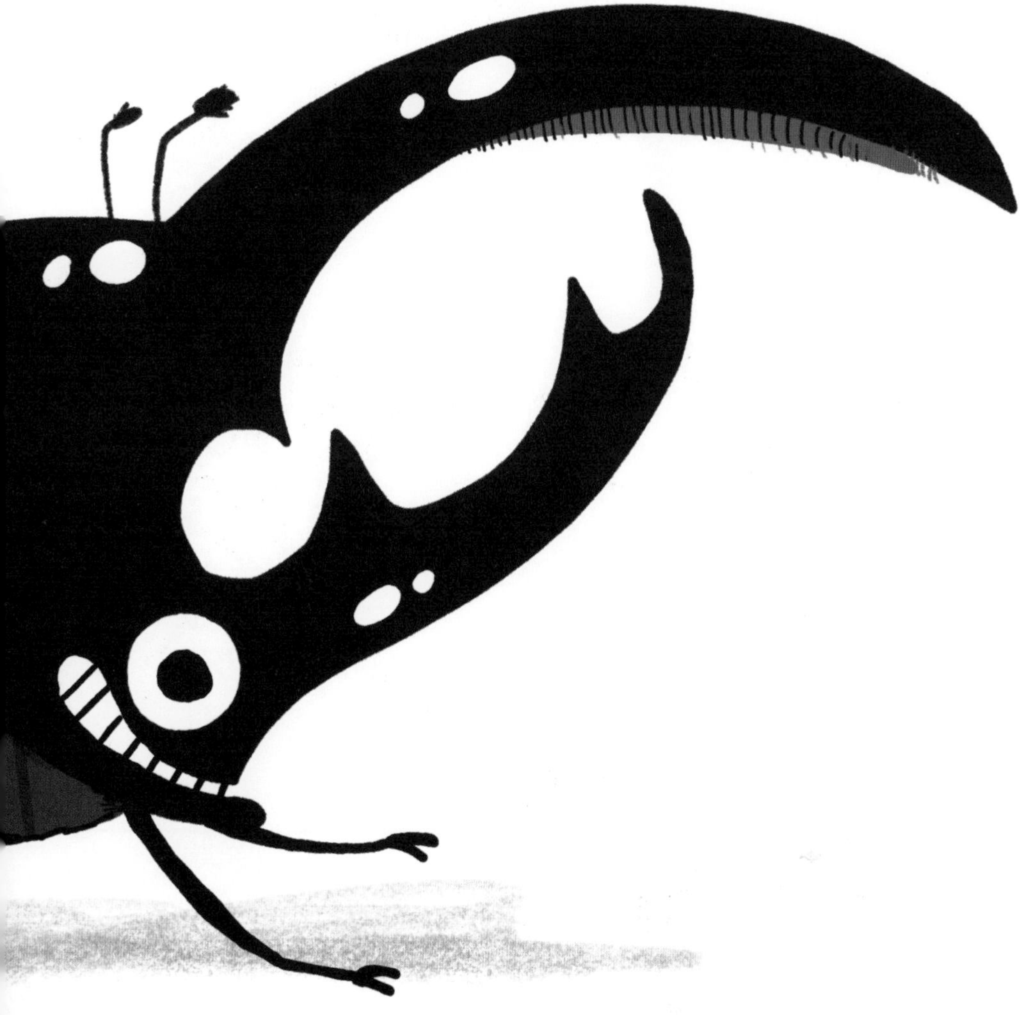

A kid once asked me what the inside of a snail looked like, and I thought it was an excellent question. I did some research and here it is:

INSIDE A SNAIL

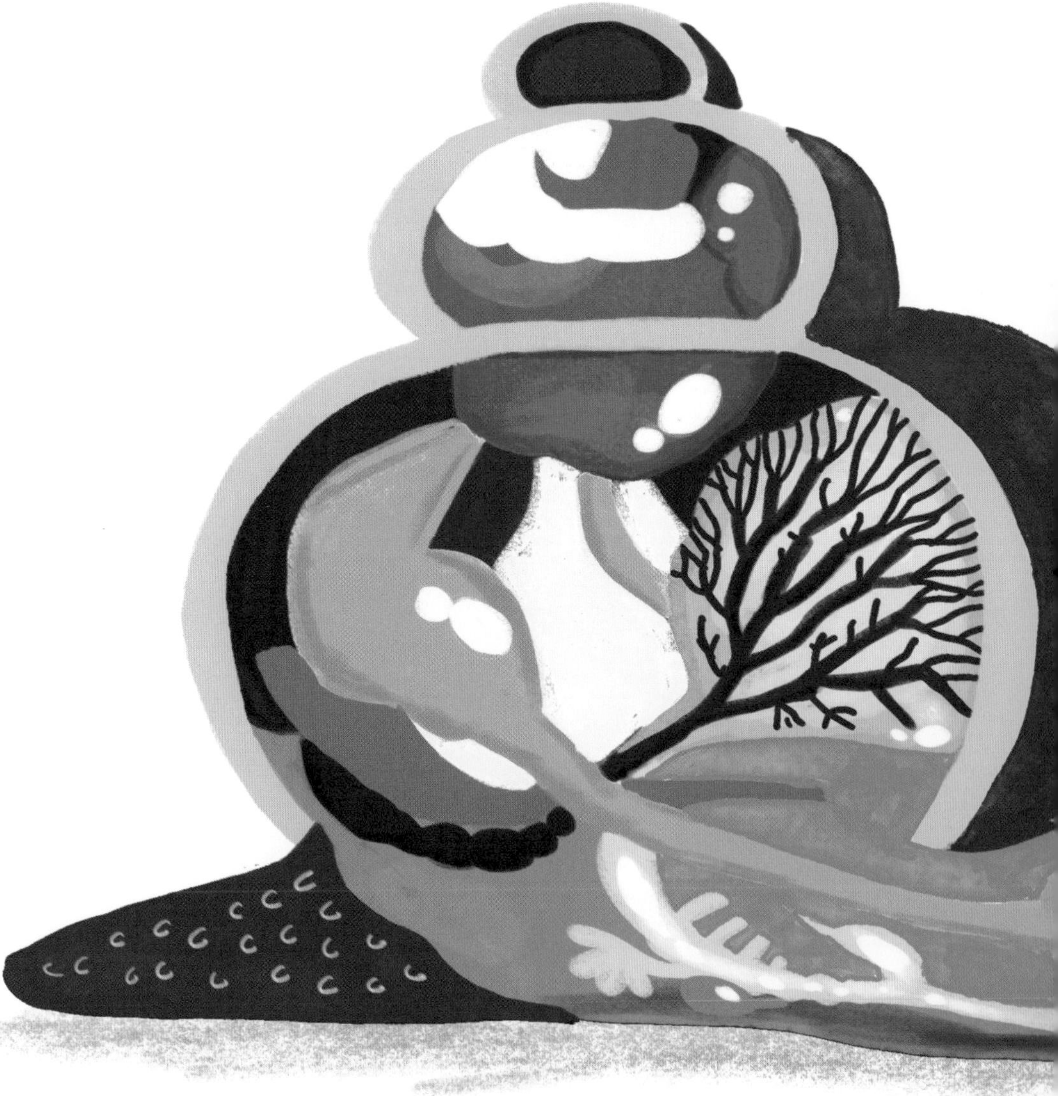

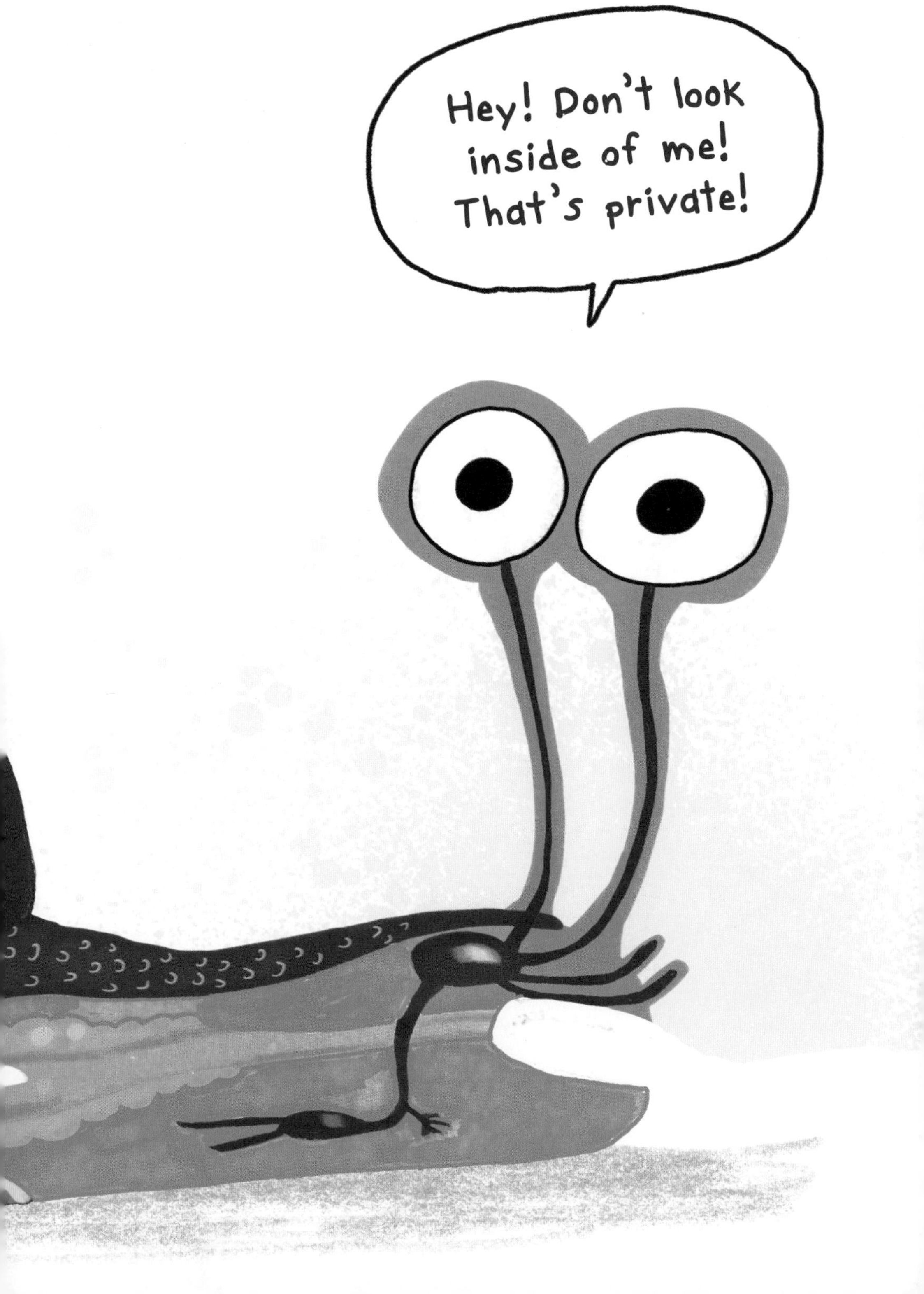
Hey! Don't look inside of me! That's private!

SOME FUN BUG FACTS

Here are some cool things I learned while researching this book:

Ladybugs can eat 5,000 insects in their lifetime!

The first creatures to go to outer space were fruit flies, and believe it or not, they came back alive!

Pill bugs are older than dinosaurs.

You're just a baby!
Pff

Caterpillars have twelve eyes.

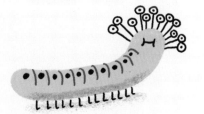

Mosquitoes are attracted to smelly feet.

Ooh, yummy!

Honeybees have hair on their eyes.

MORE FUN FACTS

Butterflies smell with their feet.

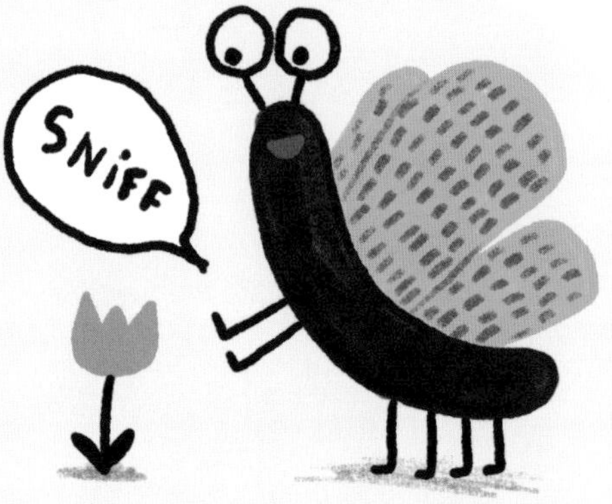
SNIFF

Grasshoppers have ears on their bellies.

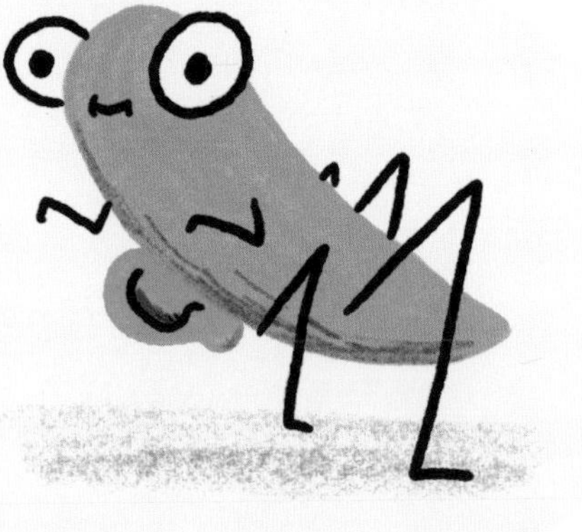

We can find bugs all over the planet, even in Antarctica, but not in the ocean.

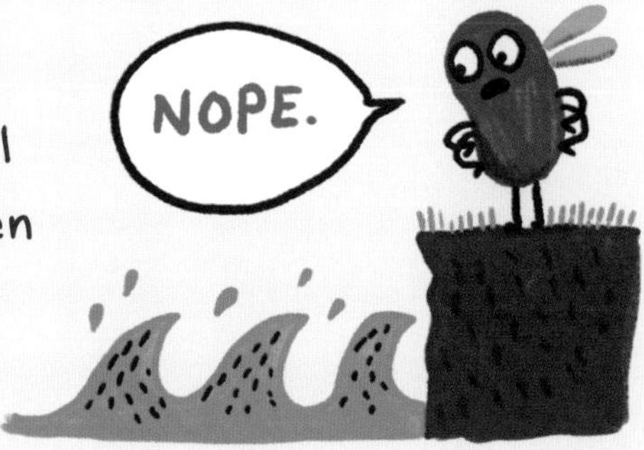
NOPE.

Snails can sleep for up to three years!

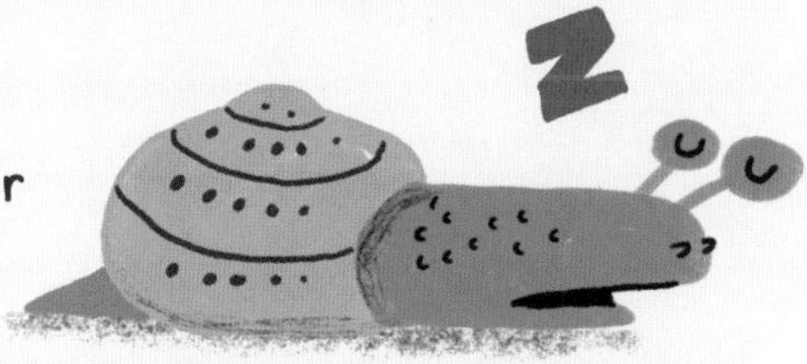

Earthworms have ten hearts! (They are not like human hearts, but they do pump blood.)

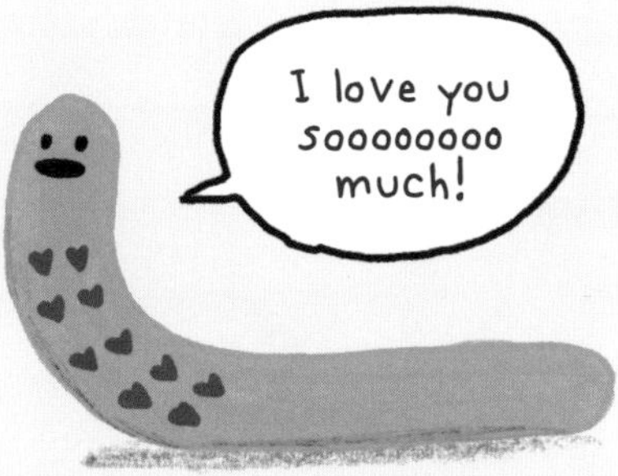
I love you soooooooo much!

Cockroaches can survive for a week without their heads.

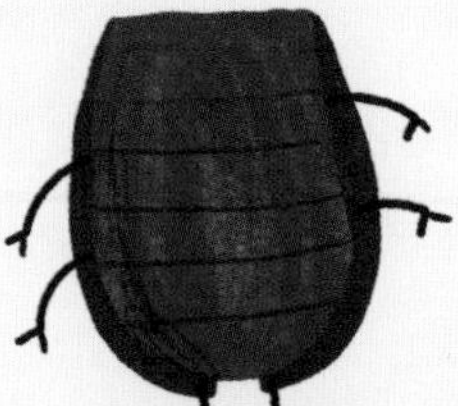

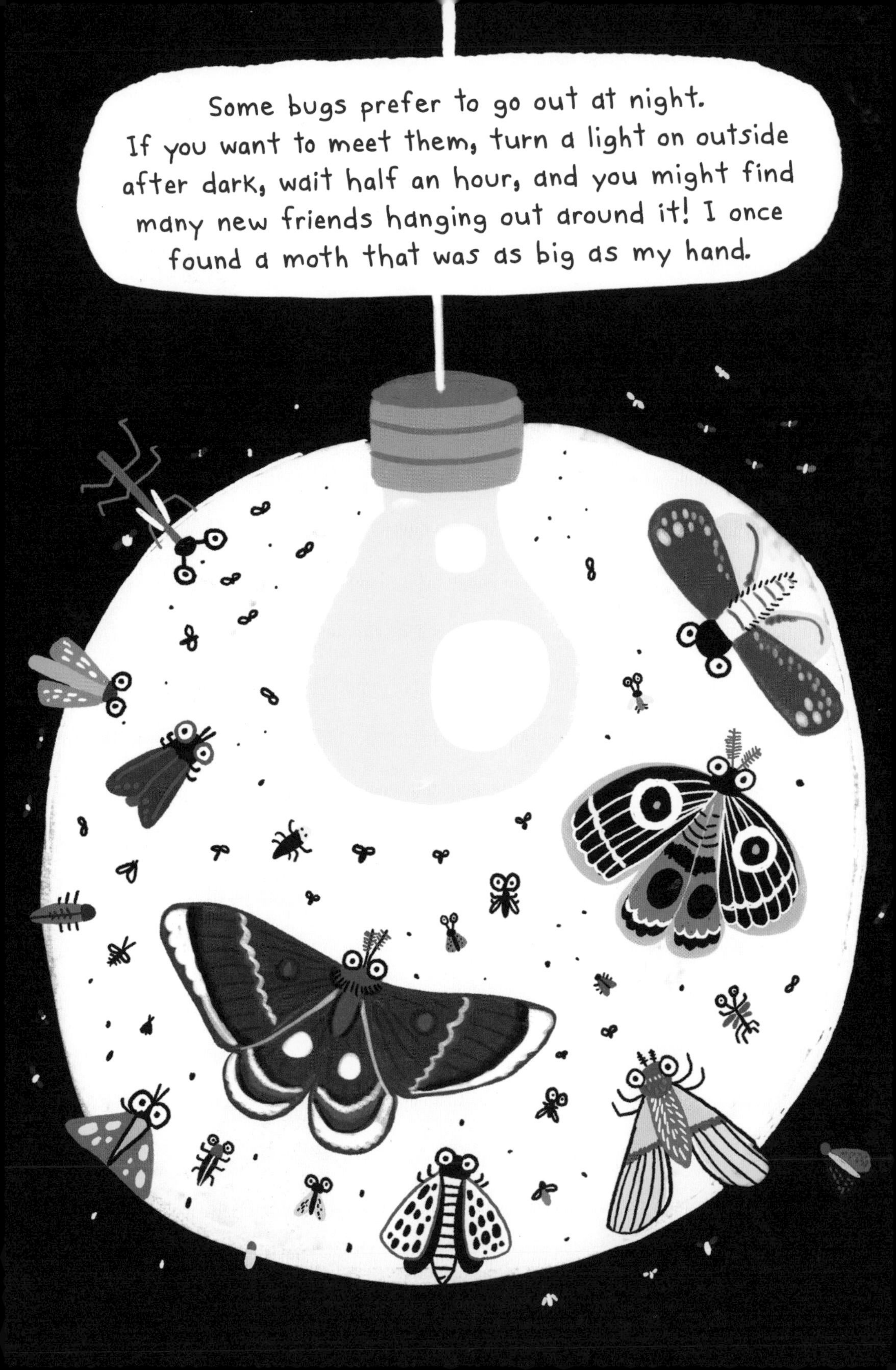
Some bugs prefer to go out at night. If you want to meet them, turn a light on outside after dark, wait half an hour, and you might find many new friends hanging out around it! I once found a moth that was as big as my hand.

Here's something I liked to do when I was a kid: I'd plant four sticks in the grass to form a square, and then try to count all the tiny bugs I could find in there. When I was done, I'd just move my sticks somewhere else and start over!

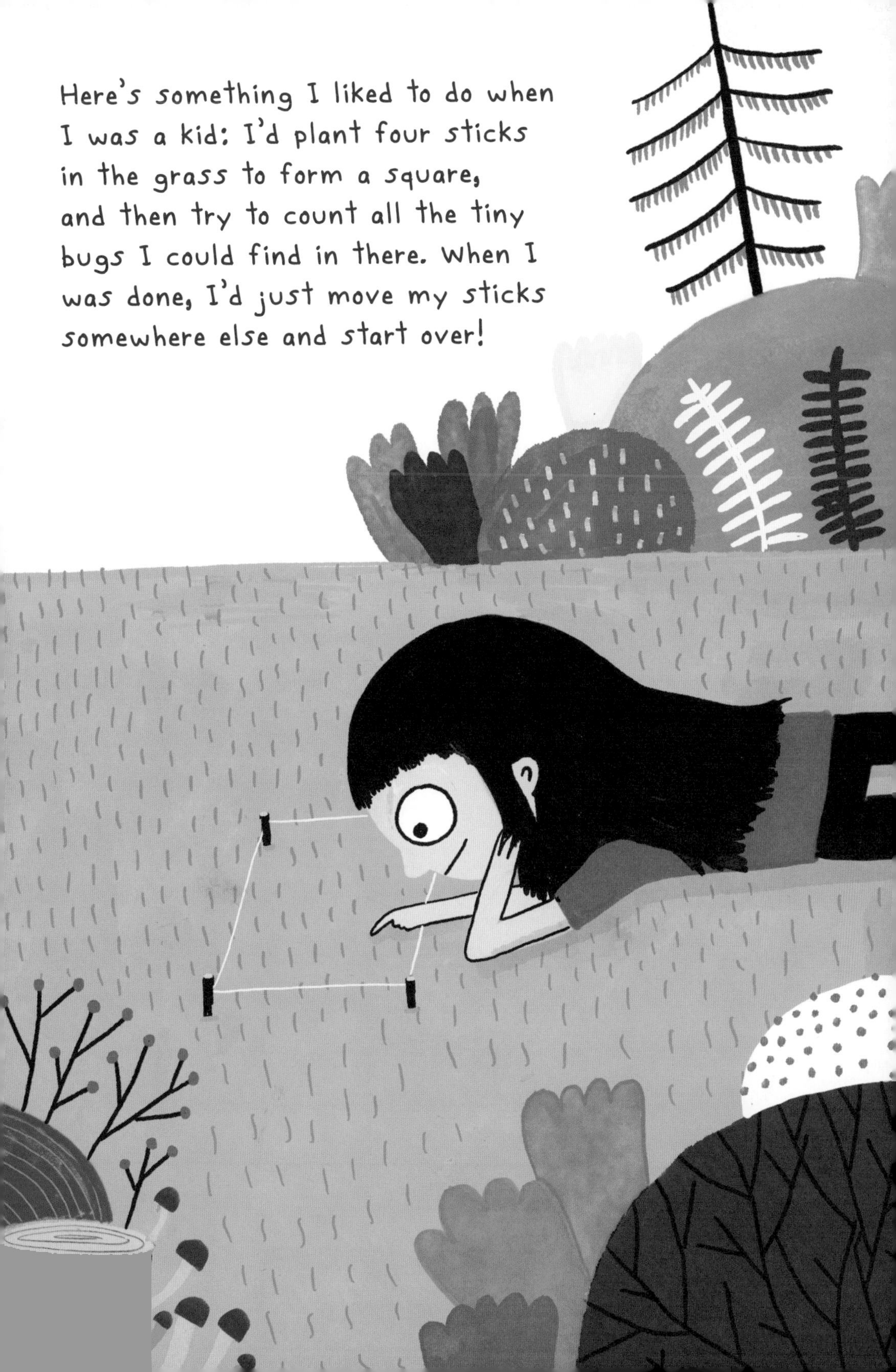

IMAGINARY BUGS

Look, I love bugs so much that I invented some! Maybe they exist somewhere on another planet, who knows?

Can you invent imaginary bugs too?

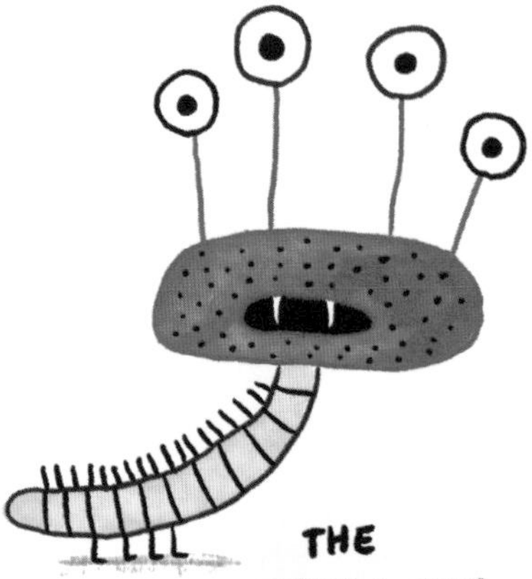
THE SUPUKLUSUS

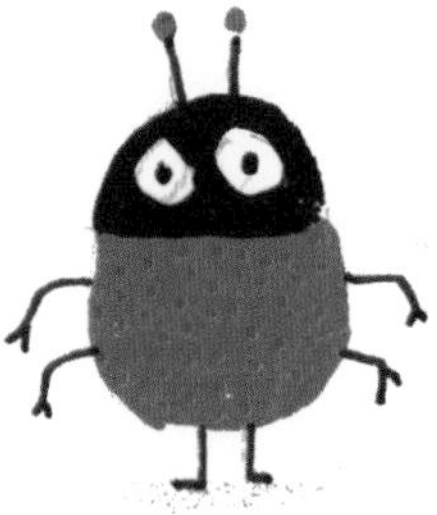
THE FRILLY GUK

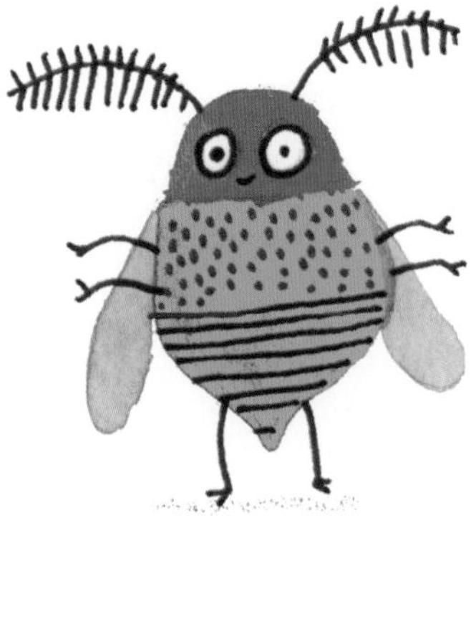
THE BOPHOPPER

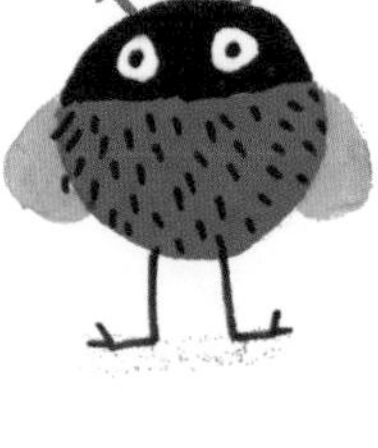
THE BAPNUS

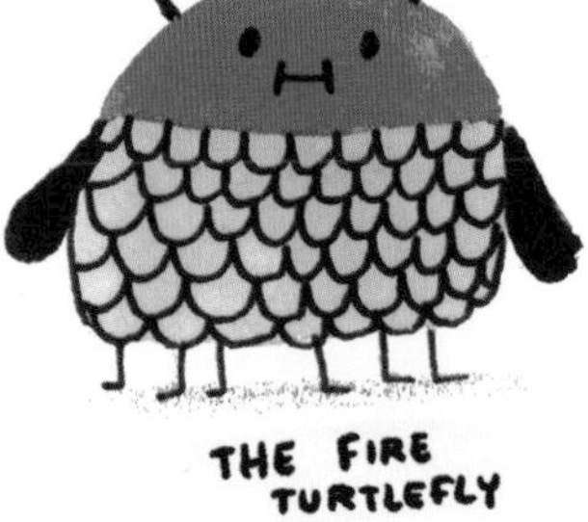
THE FIRE TURTLEFLY

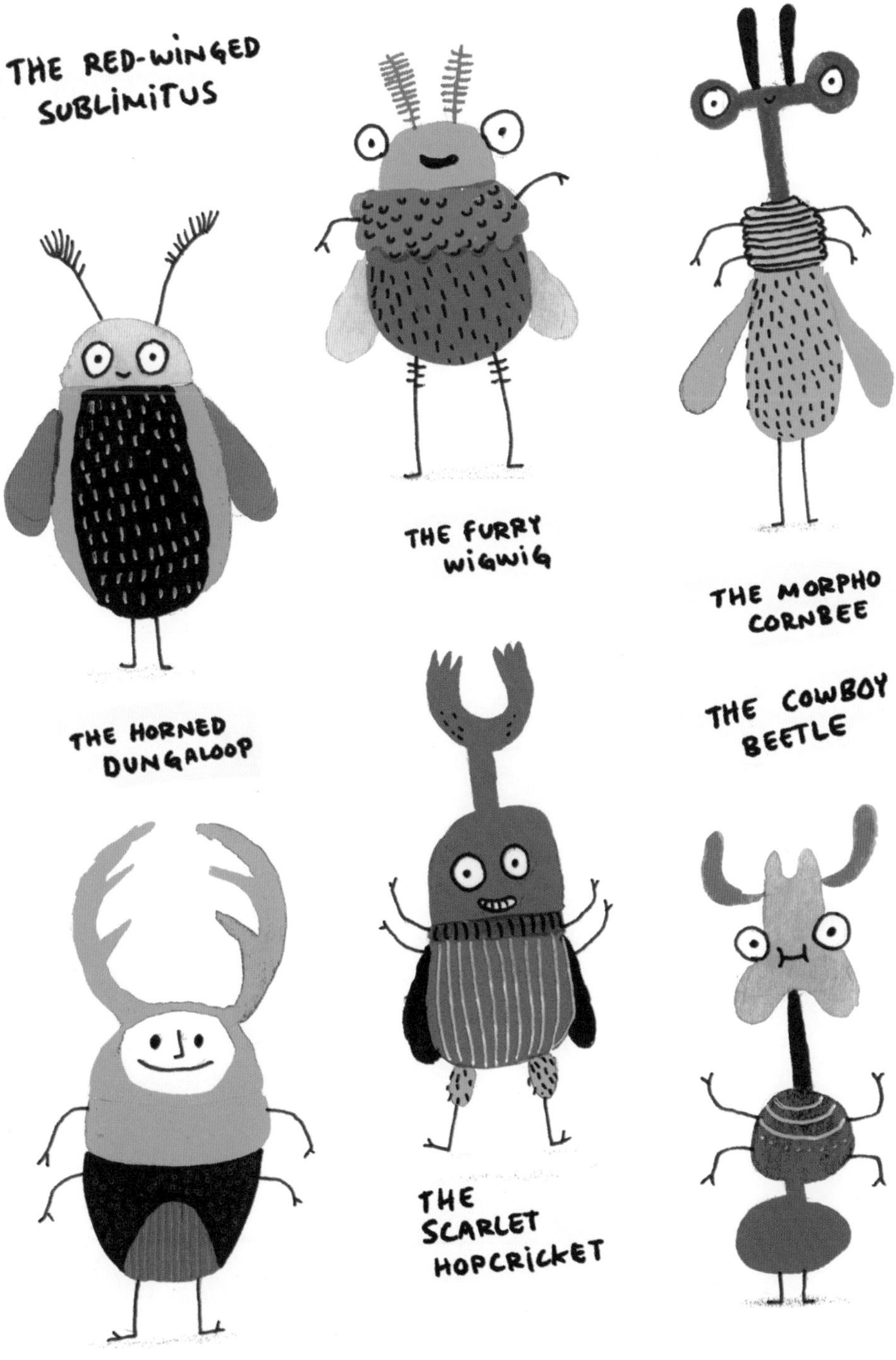
THE RED-WINGED SUBLIMITUS
THE FURRY WIGWIG
THE MORPHO CORNBEE
THE HORNED DUNGALOOP
THE COWBOY BEETLE
THE SCARLET HOPCRICKET

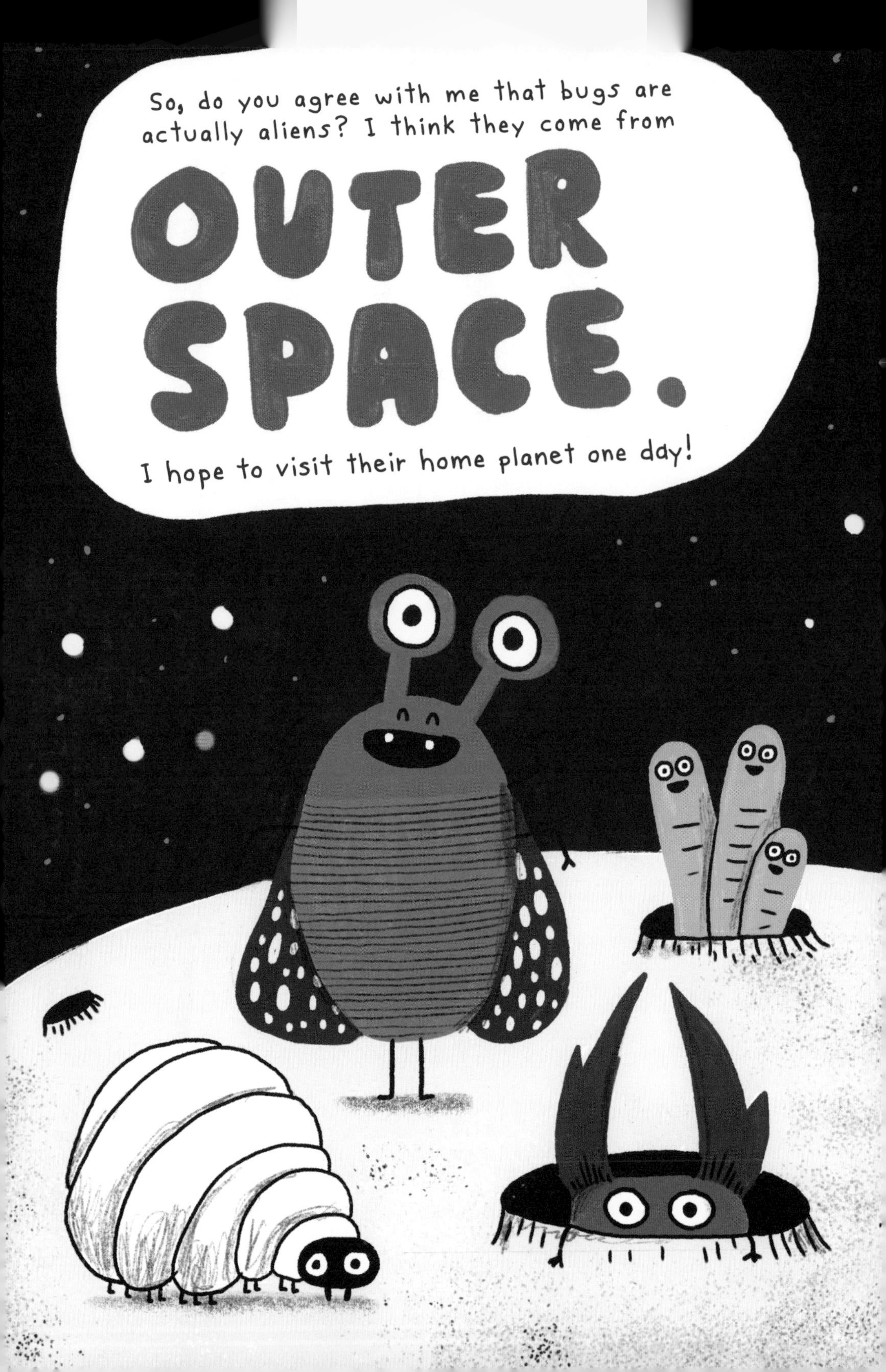
So, do you agree with me that bugs are actually aliens? I think they come from
OUTER SPACE.
I hope to visit their home planet one day!

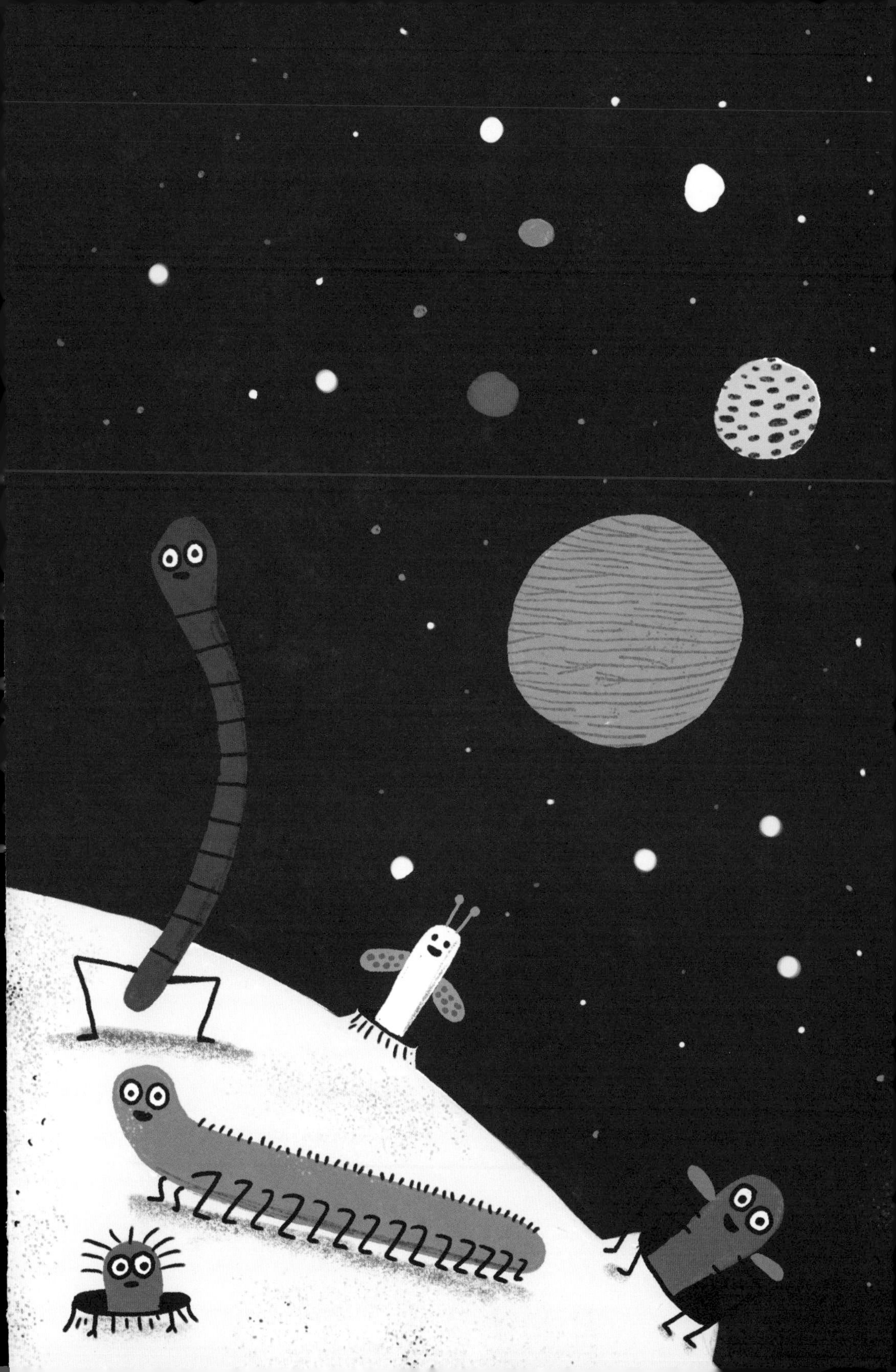
sZZZZZZZZZZZZZZZZZzzz

ELISE GRAVEL is an author/illustrator from Montreal, Quebec. After studying Graphic Design, Gravel pursued a career writing and illustrating children's books, where her quirky and charming characters quickly won the hearts of children and adults worldwide. In 2012, Gravel received the Governor General's Literary Award for her book *La clé à molette*. A prolific artist, she currently has over thirty children's books to her name, which have been translated into a dozen languages, including *The Mushroom Fan Club*, *The Worst Book Ever*, and *If Found Please Return to Elise Gravel*, her challenge to young artists to keep a sketchbook. Elise Gravel lives in Montreal with her spouse, two daughters, cats, and a few spiders.

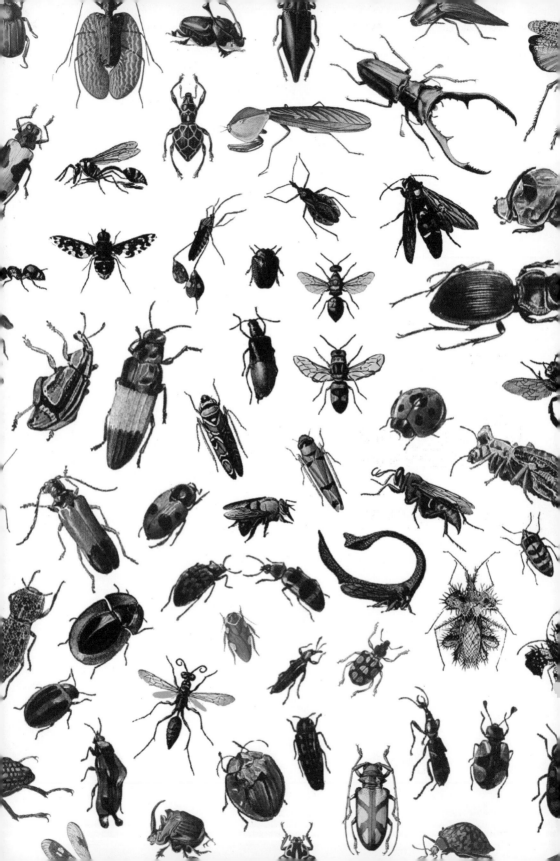